OF STARDUST
A QUEER, FANTASTICAL ANTHOLOGY
AVRAH C. BAREN

CHAOS MONSTER PUBLISHING

Cover design © Fantastical Ink

Edited by Lillian Barry

Published by Chaos Monster Publishing LLC

ISBN 979-8-9900546-3-9 (paperback)

ISBN 979-8-9900546-2-2 (ebook)

CONTENTS

For you, you beautiful creatures of star-stuff and magic.

Preface

In 2023, I attended Pride for the first time. I was 32. I looked around the world, at crowds of people covered in all the colors of the rainbow, and thought to myself: "We need more of this." More rainbows, and glitter, and queer joy in all its complicated forms. I turned to my writing community and asked, "Shall we?" And eight beautiful authors said, "Hell yes!"

When I came out in the midst of a pandemic (I know, I know, who didn't?), I wasn't sure what I would do with this new information about myself. Would I let myself be queer? Would I tell anyone? Would I ever sit in on meetings of the LGBTQ+ group at work and feel like anything other than an outsider?

I didn't know. For years I'd been calling myself "mostly straight." It was more of a joke than anything else. It took me a long time to figure out that those words held weight. And when I did, I thought, "Maybe this is knowledge I keep to myself." It was a valid choice, and one I could make for myself.

And then I sat in a chair backwards and a friend said, "That's so stereotypically bi," and I stammered out a "So...about that."

It was just those two friends at first. Two of my closest friends in a cabin in the middle of a pandemic as we wondered if life would ever look "normal" again. And since then my whole world has shifted. Since then I've come out to friends who have said, "Well, yeah, didn't you already tell me?" Who knew I was queer before *I* knew I was queer. I joined queer, Jewish groups in the city. I live with a friend I found through those same groups. I started writing my queerness into my stories. I found other queer writers to share those stories with.

This is only one story among many. There's no one way, there's no *right* way to be queer. There's a world in which I would have stayed closeted and still been queer. There's a world in which I would be in a hetero-presenting relationship and still be queer. I love that queerness means so many different things. If you look at our community, if you tilt it to the right light, you see not only rainbows, but prisms of light.

This collection is much the same. Tilt it one way and you see unabashed joy. Tilt it another and there's rage. Another, and suddenly you're lightyears away, contemplating your past and future.

We wrote these stories in a time where we were aching for more queer stories out in the world, where the world was hurting us. It's still hurting us. We still ache for these stories. It's too common to read the news and watch people you've never met paint broad strokes about who you are, who your community is, why you should be condemned for existing and loving and thriving. We grieve the lives lost. We hurt, but we fight. They try to erase us and instead we burn brighter than ever.

We will keep writing these stories. I hope this is the first of many collections of Stardust stories. Because we are here and vibrant and *we* are made of star stuff. And we are damned well going to shine.

What you hold in your hands is a collection of stories that are full of queerness and dreaming. You hold your own bit of stardust. There is joy and confusion and grief and discovery. There are open doors through which you can peek your head in to find a tired cyborg or a calculator obsessed with shiny things. There are rainweavers and sentient plants, dark libraries and strange seas. Catch the nearest falling star, sprinkle on some glitter, and we'll meet you where the rainbow is just beginning.

The Dugong Wife and the Raincape Weaver

Gabriella Buba

He brought her home in his karakoa, the gleaming polished prow of the war-boat seeming dull compared to the way the sun gleamed off her blue-black hair and in her huge glistening brown eyes.

It was not unusual for a rich and powerful ruler like our Datu to have brought a wife home so, draped in a net of gold from head to toe, her palanquin shaded by palm leaves, two attendants fanning her as the rowers strained at their posts, bearing her over the cresting turquoise waves like the rare treasure she was. She might have been from the islands of Mindinao or Sulu, a princess of one of the Great Rajanates or Sultanates of the South, or perhaps the daughter of a hero-chieftain of Ibalon.

But no, Lady Luha of Luzon, as the Dayang came to be known, did not come from *across* the sea, but *from* it. Even the pounds of gold our Datu draped about her neck and wrists in ever more costly chains paled in comparison to the golden hue of her warm brown skin, like sunlight gleaming on the shallow waters over seagrass beds. But even chains of gold cannot keep a dugong wife from the waves, though he tried, how he tried.

For five years he kept her at his side and no amount of ill luck that befell him would convince him of his folly. First came the red tide in waves that kept our fishermen's boats beached for weeks. The next year there came a great typhoon out of season. Damaged fruits and ruined harvests rotted sweetly in the steaming heat. We ate roots not rice. When she bore him a son at last, we thought, surely he would let her go. But no. He could not see reason when it came to her. And yet she was such a treasure that for all the island suffered, I heard not one word spoken against the lady herself.

In the fifth year Lady Luha bore a daughter who shared her luminous brown eyes in her wide round face, who they say was slipped into the world with hands webbed like fins. And something changed. Though her daughter was hale and strong, her son a laughing mercurial creature, and the Datu, her husband, ever doting, Lady Luha only wept. Her laugh silenced, her smiles gone. So they called her Luha for her tears.

A humble weaver of raincapes such as myself should never have acquainted myself with a lady so exalted and so beautiful. But that year, whether she was walking under the shade of her servants' silk umbrellas along the beach, wood-sandaled feet never quite touching the sand, tending her newborn daughter, or seated beside her husband at his banquet feasts, she wept. Her huge once luminous eyes grew puffy and red with tears which fell down her face fatter and faster than raindrops, salty as the sea. She wept so much so that the Datu commissioned me to make her a magnificent anahaw raincape to keep her tears from ruining the fine silk of her robes.

He told me that he wanted the layered and woven palm dyed with all shades of indigo from deepest near black to seagrass green, painted with powdered mother of pearl and embroidered with silver thread to resemble the cresting surf. He wanted every sort of sea creature woven in among the blue and green fronds, turtles and puffer fish, seahorses, rabbitfish and rays. Most of all, embroidered in silver thread upon the back, a dugong, caught in a golden net.

The payment he promised was a fortune, enough that my family would never feel the pinch of hunger even should greater disasters befall our island. And the chance to display my best craft upon his most admired lady would bring yet more business. It had to be perfect.

So I began. For weeks I worked over my finest dried palm fronds, painting and dying, cutting and weaving, indigo, turquoise, and sun-bleached palm fronds dipped in mother of pearl under my callused fingertips became rows and rows of crashing waves, calm cerulean waters and waving seagrass. I wove until my fingers ached and my eyes burned, till I had a cape fit for a Dayang.

The Datu sent his best warriors and fisher folk to the reefs and shallows to bring me samples of every sea creature so that I could match their hue, the shape of their scales, and the color of their gleaming fins. All that I lacked was the dugong, for it was taboo to hunt them, even for a man as great as our Datu. We needed no further reason for ill luck to visit itself upon us. The Datu told me to save the dugong for last, with its pounds of silver and gold thread, till after his wife had approved of her gift.

"Weaver Halina with a gift for the Dayang."

The introduction rang in my ears as I knelt before the low dais in the feasting hall, and at last presented my creation to Lady Luha, nestled in its woven box of nipa. But before her beauty the turquoise of the waves paled beside the blue-black shadows of her hair. My seahorses and darting fish looked dead-eyed, the gleam of their silver-edged scales false and garish in comparison to the moon of her face glistening with tears.

I apologized, and apologized again, my cheeks red with shame, promising I would return to the Datu all the silver thread and the price of his costly dyes.

The Datu waved me off. His proud face turned toward his warriors, already bored of the joke, but then Lady Luha laid a gold-encrusted hand on the back of his. Her rings, heavy and dotted with coral, were as pink and lush as her lips.

"Asawa ko, I have taken a liking to the pattern of her weaving and the hue of her dyes. Let me take over this commission." Her voice was low and melodious, gentle as the lapping of waves on shore.

Every ear bent to hear it in the crowded feasting hall, including mine.

The Datu's iron-wood dark cheeks creased in a smile. He raised her ringed hand and kissed her fingers. "Mahal, I have not seen you take such an interest in months. The weaver is yours."

Lady Luha rose then, tears dripping from her chin at the motion; she beckoned to me and I stumbled over myself to trot at her heels, clutching my now tawdry-seeming cape in trembling hands. We adjourned to her private rooms, gauzed and draped in white and indigo lace and translucent piña cloth such that we seemed to slip underwater, the sounds of the feasting distant and muffled.

She led me through her apartments, onto a private pier that extended into a nook of a cove that I, who had lived on this island my entire life, had never seen.

The water lay so still and clear that at first I mistook it for a freshwater fishpond, till I saw it was not gourami or tilapia sending shimmering shocks of moonlight through the water but dizzyingly colored tropical fish darting among the seagrass. Dozens of oil lamps hung from the top of a bamboo fence built several meters out around the pier. They filled the salty air with a warm glow and the scent of ylang-ylang.

"How—?" The question strangled in my throat but the lady pointed one long-fingered hand to the far side of the water where volcanic walls of stone plunged into the sea, and there, just where low tide had begun to expose it, was a low arch of stone... a sea cave, no. A tunnel, one of the lava tunnels that must connect this little pocket cove to the sea, one which might never be revealed except when the tide was at its lowest.

When Lady Lahu knelt down on a tasseled cushion on the edge of the pier, I dropped to my knees behind her, wincing at the loud hollow thump of my knees on bamboo. She was so graceful I could not even hear her footfalls, only the gentle clink of her gold jewelry.

I bent low and clutched my cape to my chest, feeling the palm fronds rustle and crinkle in my sweating grip.

"May I see it again?" The Lady's voice was warmer now, so close it half seemed I could feel her breath on my hot cheeks.

I fumbled my creation forward, spreading it before her, unrolling it from its wrappings so she could see the full three-quarter circle flat upon the bamboo pier. In the face of her impossible beauty I was acutely aware of each frayed palm leaf, and every off-color strand, each crooked stitch. Every mistake gilded in lamplight. I wanted to sink it beneath stones to the bottom of the cove for the fish to nibble on.

I tore my gaze away from her rapt inspection back to the water, where I locked eyes with a huge saltwater crocodile, just outside the bamboo lattice. Only its glowing golden eyes were above the water; the flickering of fish and oil-lights shimmering on the surface had disguised their predatory gleam.

"We'll start here," Lady Luha said at last, her voice dragging me free from the crocodile's cold reptilian gaze.

I looked to find her pearldust-dipped nails grazing over a seahorse I had woven into the cape, its annatto orange tail coiled around a stalk of seagrass.

"They prefer shallow water and are not particularly skittish," she added. "Come tomorrow morning, near high tide."

"I hope I will do the work justice this time," I promised her.

She blinked her big wet eyes at me. "A less skilled artist would have fared better. You so faithfully recorded every detail, you even captured the dead-eyed glint and scales drying in the sun. I should like to be seen so clearly."

The next day Lady Luha had three of the island's many chickens in a basket on the dock. She hurled it with a flick of her delicate wrist out past the bamboo lattice to the center of the lagoon.

The yellow-eyed saltwater crocodile emerged from his lair, beside the mouth of the sea-tunnel that connected this lagoon to the ocean, and swallowed them up in one bite, basket and all. Then he retreated back into the shadow of the volcanic cliffs on the far side of the lagoon, silvery bubbles steaming from his toothy snout as he went.

He must have been twenty feet long, with a splotched pattern of black and gold up his tail that gave way to an impenetrable black hide broken only by white teeth each as long as my palm.

I stared in apprehension, but Lady Luha was pointing her full pink lips toward a ladder on the edge of the pier.

"He won't approach?" I asked; I couldn't imagine that three chickens would be enough to satisfy such a creature.

"Not after eating, and not inside the fence. Even my boy swims here once the buwaya has been fed." She had her daughter nursing at her high golden breast, her endless tears leaving wet splotches on the infant's downy black hair.

I went into the water. The warm cerulean water lapped at my ankles, then my knees, then my hips. I balked at going any deeper or further from the ladder. Luckily, the Lady smiled at me and instructed that I was deep enough and should stand very still and inspect the seagrass tangling around my calves.

I could not tear my eyes away from where silvery bubbles still disturbed the glassy surface of the lagoon. I might've stood petrified as wood till low tide until a small warm hand landed on the back of my neck and pushed.

Lady Luha had reached over the edge of the pier to direct my attention downward. I bent at her gentle nudge, my heart in my throat at the softness of her palm, the shape of her beautiful lips around my name.

"Halina?"

Could she feel how much sweat had gathered at my nape?

But then I couldn't think about such things any longer, for she had bent me forward till my shadow lay over the water below me, creating a clear window free of the concealing shimmer of sunlight, a window into an underwater world come alive.

The first seahorses I saw were bright orange, spiny tails curled around the base of the seagrass to anchor themselves, but the longer I looked the more I saw, tiny ones that were pink and knobbed all over, the patterning concealing them against the sandy bottom. Big yellow ones that at first I mistook for strands of seagrass themselves. I watched as the sun beat down on the back of my neck and my fingers itched to weave.

I only left the water when my toes had pruned and the Datu's youngest child had been taken away by her nurse, and the crocodile rose from his rest at the bottom of the lagoon and began swimming along the edge of the bamboo lattice keeping him away from the pier.

Only Lady Luha remained outside, resting in her pillowed seating area under a palm umbrella her servants had erected. She sat, eyes closed, tears squeezing down her cheeks and darkening the turquoise blue of her robe to indigo.

Her deep brown eyes opened when I dragged myself on wobbly knees up the ladder, my legs having forgotten how to support my weight. She smiled and patted the cushions beside her.

I demurred, not wanting to ruin such fine fabric with salt water.

At my protest she laughed aloud, the sound of it like surf on a pebbled beach. "My husband no longer gifts me things which will be ruined by salt water." She gestured to her tear-wet robe: "Jute stone beaten till it's nearly as soft as silk."

I sat at the very edge of the shade. "I will begin weaving as soon as I return to my workshop. I will have to go to the palengke for fresh turmeric and—"

I froze when Lady Luha reached out, drawing her fingertips down my bare arm, collecting the droplets of salt water beading on my skin. She'd lifted her hand halfway to her coral pink lips as if she intended to lick the salt water from her fingertips before the crocodile let out a low croaking rumble. We both snatched ourselves back, her eyes darting wide and terrified towards the behemoth at the center of the lagoon. She might even have flushed.

"Not turmeric; we will take one of the Datu's boats. I will show you where to dive for a special kind of kelp." She picked up the conversation as if nothing strange had passed at all.

And so it went. In the mornings I waded and swam around the dock observing all manner of sea creatures that came to the lagoon as if on a pilgrimage to greet a great queen. Her offerings to the great crocodile became larger, until she fed him a whole pig. He ate so well that day I saw him leave his preferred place at the center of the lagoon and drag himself up on the golden sands to sleep off the meal. I was left free to swim beyond the fencing, examining the constellations of patterns upon the wings of a massive ray. The Lady Luha watched, her huge eyes brimming with longing and tears, but she never left the pier. Never even trailed her hand into the lapping waves. She only touched salt water if it gathered on my skin or hair, when I would emerge, to report all I had seen.

In the afternoons I would follow Lady Luha's advice on where to obtain the best dyes touched by the sea. She unlocked the wealth of the sea before my very eyes. Indigo from marshy wetlands where the influx of salt gave a broader range of color, seaweed in dozens of hues, a type of shell crushed into thread that was more perfectly pearlescent for scales than silver. Even the Anahaw palm I harvested fresh, from the center of a dense mangrove forest where palms had found ways to live atop mangrove roots amid the coming and the going of the tide. Hers would be a cape that was as much of the sea as she was.

At night, under the light of dozens of oil lamps filled with ylang-ylang-scented coconut oil, I wove the cape anew. Under her watchful eye the tapestry under my fingertips came alive as nothing I'd created before. I wove the cape in two layers, the exterior woven of anahaw showing a sunlit seascape, the inside of thick shining silk, showing how the lagoon and its denizens changed at night. At the back I embroidered the silver dugong in its golden net, and inside was Lady Luha herself, dressed only in her endless ropes of gold and precious stones. I worked on the lady's visage in secret even from her, holding her tear-wet face in my mind as I transfixed her image onto the deep indigo lining, speckled with the reflection of stars and moonlight on midnight waters.

I hardly slept, yet at her beck and call, I came alive as never before. My skin ripened into a deeper tea-dark hue in the sun. My hair's constant taming of coconut oil washed away and it became wavy as the playful surf in which I spent half my time.

We went on so for three months and I should have been happy to continue so forever. Indeed, the cloak had been complete for a week or more. I only dithered over the details, tweaking and perfecting them, drawing out our time together as long as I could.

I spent hours studying how the tear-tracks on her face glimmered in the moonlight and how the shape of her brows arched like the curl of a gentle wave. I stitched till my hands shook and my eyesight grew dim with exhaustion. But still I did not waver from my lady's side nor beg a day's reprieve from her tutelage.

Until the day the crocodile did not emerge from his lair to consume his offering of one of the Datu's prized horses, who had broken a leg and had to be put down.

The servants who had dragged today's offering to the very edge of the sand, nearest the volcanic cliffs on the far side of the lagoon, had gone on their way quickly. Everyone had long ago tired of our study of the lagoon and all its myriad denizens. Even the Lady's boy had tired of watching our game, which never changed, and the nursemaid of sitting out on the pier.

We were alone, but for the watchful yellow eyes of the crocodile.

We both waited, watching the beast where he rested on a small ledge in a deep crack in the cliff walls, well fed and sleeping, just beside the opening to the sea-tunnel, his black hide seeming deeper than the shadows of his lair. He did not move. His great golden eyes did not even flicker at the scent of blood which rose from the carcass not five feet away.

The Lady walked slowly to the end of the pier and sat, her legs dangling, her toes dipping into the water. The crocodile did not stir.

I do not have words for how her face changed then. She had always been beautiful, but something came alive behind her soulful grieving eyes that I could not name.

Lady Luha turned to me. "Halina, is the cape finished?"

"Yes, Lady," I assured her, the truth easy as air now that I could see that at last the brightness in her eyes was not tears. There was no need to draw out my labors a moment longer. "It is a masterpiece."

"A fitting exchange then, one treasure for another." She beckoned to me and we dove into the lagoon.

I followed her, past the bamboo lattice fence, and across the seagrass bed that filled the calm water of the lagoon. My eyes were well used to seeing underwater, my limbs grown strong and sure in swimming, such that I could keep with Lady Luha, hampered as she was by her draping robe and chains of gold. If I had thought she looked beautiful before, it was nothing to how she looked in her element. The waves embraced her as the sun never could, as the Datu with his gold and wealth never could. As I wished I could. The rainbow of darting rabbitfish swirled around her, their bodies glinting like jewels.

I caught up with her halfway across the lagoon and helped her free herself from her entanglements. Gleaming golden piña fiber robes floated up to the surface of the water. Pearls and coral, gold chains, bangles, arm-cuffs, and earrings sank down to the sand.

She led me deeper into the shadow of the volcanic cliffs on the far side of the Lagoon, towards the sea-tunnel that led towards the ocean, towards her freedom. Towards the sleeping reptilian guardian who kept her here.

We surfaced for air in the shadow of the cliffs, with the current of the sea-tunnel tugging greedy fingertips at our legs.

"My Lady?" I whispered it, afraid to draw the attention of the beast lounging on the ledge nearby. The rumble of its sleeping breaths sent ripples across the water, a fetid funk perfuming the air with death.

She turned to me, her eyes gone strange, but so alive. I was held in her gaze, transfixed. She gathered my face in her hands, drawing me so close I could feel her breath on my lips. "My sea name is Bulawan and my skin is weighed down in his lair. Will you help me retrieve it? I cannot enter. If I do it will surely wake the beast, no matter how well fed he is. But you, he's grown so accustomed to you, my dear Halina."

I would have agreed to anything in that moment. Even with the reptilian stench of crocodile in my nose, and the dead horse bloating in the sun, nothing mattered but Bulawan, my lady of tears no more. She ought to be freed, her to the sea, and my island of the weight of her ill luck.

I nodded and she kissed me, pressing the air from her lungs into mine, till my head swam and my blood felt like it was full of starlight. When she pushed me under the water, my lungs ached only with longing and not for want of air.

I dove, not wanting to waste a moment of my lady's gift, down into the crocodile's lair. The color of the water shifted around me, leaving the cerulean sunlit waters of the shallow lagoon; the world became shades of indigo and black. I pulled myself into the massive fissure in the lava. The sharp stone cut into my hands, my blood clouding the water.

Icy fear slithered down my spine. I had to be quick. Nothing drew the crocodile's attention like fresh spilled blood. I swam deeper, careful now to avoid the razor edges of the craggy walls, in and down, till the pressure of the water beat against my eardrums. Nothing lived here, no silver minnows sheltered amongst the cracks in the walls and no oysters or mussels clung to the black rock.

At first it seemed I would find nothing but more knife-sharp volcanic rocks and the picked-clean bones of old prey, and then ahead the darkness of the fissure changed. A strange silvery light illuminated the deepest part of the crevasse. Then I saw it, my lady's dugong skin. It seemed to glow like the full moon on the water, and it was weighed down by a large anchor stone.

My lungs had finally begun to feel tight with want of air and the great pressure of this depth, but I could not return empty-handed. I swam down, grasping the bored-out hole of the anchor stone and bracing my bare feet against the sides of the fissure as I attempted to shift the stone. But even with the aid of the water it was too heavy for me, though I tugged until my feet bled from the press of the sharp volcanic walls.

As I tugged, precious bubbles of shared breath escaped my lips and I could feel the gift of my lady's kiss being spent too quickly.

After one particularly desperate tug, my hands flew loose from the anchor stone and I flung myself back into the wall of the crevasse; bones scattered and tumbled down around me. I seized a femur, large enough to come from a carabao, my flesh crawling at the algae-slick texture, but I jammed the end under the anchor stone and levered it up with all my strength. At first it seemed the bone would only sink down into the sand, but then I felt the bottom edge catch, and the huge anchor began to roll. As precious silvery bubbles streamed away with each heave of exertion, finally, finally the anchor stone rolled free of the shimmering dugong skin.

I snatched up my prize and swam desperately for the surface and the open sunlit water of the lagoon, blood streaming behind me into the dark waters, suffusing the crocodile's lair with my scent. He would surely know it had been me who stole the treasure he had been tasked to guard. The Datu and his katalonan, who had charmed the beast to his task, would surely know.

Just as the last silvery bubbles of air streamed out of my nose, my lungs screaming for air, I burst free of the crack, into the lagoon, face to face with the crocodile himself.

I screamed, saw the last of my air race for the surface without me, as the crocodile lunged, maw agape—

Sure hands caught me up and dragged me aside as the crocodile barreled past me into its lair, its long tail lashing the water to froth. Bulawan and I shot through the sea-tunnel as if dragged by a rip-tide, toward the distant freedom of open water.

As the darkness closed over our heads, spots danced before my eyes, lack of air finally taking its toll. I felt her lips press over mine once more, her hands closing on the precious treasure in my grasp.

Unbury Yourself
Avrah C. Baren

Ground shaking beneath my roots. The tread of a trespasser scatters jays and doves from my arms. Sunlight slips between canopy leaves to alight on a stranger.

A young man, pale of skin, wide of eye as he discovers me, large of smile as he stares.

"You're real," he murmurs.

I keep my arms stretched towards the sun, reveling in the warmth of it upon my bark and phylum flesh, the small breeze teasing the leaves of hair. Perhaps the jays will return and I might feast upon one when it has become too trusting. Tear into its flesh with sharp teeth.

The man steps closer. The creak of branches as I snap my head towards him. He freezes, blue eyes huge in his skull, golden hair reflecting the golden afternoon.

"I mean no harm. It is only that I'm a botanist, you see. A scholar of plants. And you, you are the most fascinating one I've ever heard tale of."

"Leave, scholar of plants," I say. His voice is musical. Mine is the voice of the woods itself. The sway of branches. The cry of a hawk. Musical in a different way. "Leave, or perhaps I shall feast upon your bones."

The man pales further, skin snow-white and nearly lifeless.

"I came with a gift," he says.

"Then leave your gift and go," I mutter. My attention is for the open sky. The snuffling of a deer nearby. This human is nothing but a trespasser.

The man bends down, just out of reach, for I am tethered to the place of my birthing. The vine that extends from my torso into the earth is plain for all to see. But one step more and I could have him.

He empties something from his pocket, tosses it closer so I may reach it, should I choose to approach. Stands, and opens his mouth to say nothing, before fleeing beyond the bright sunlight of my grove.

When his footsteps can no longer be felt in the network of roots below, I approach this gift of his. Pick it up and examine it between the gnarled, wooden fingers of my right hand.

A feather from a bird I have never seen, iridescent greens and blues shining like a beacon. I tuck the feather in between my leaves, and return my attention to the sky.

⊛

The golden boy returns the next day. Less golden amongst the gray clouds and threatening sky. I long for rain to breach the belly of each cloud, to soak soil and root.

He watches as I finish my meal. A squirrel this time. I stood so still it skittered along my feet. Such a simple thing to snatch it and sink my teeth into its warm flesh. If the boy approaches, perhaps I will feast again.

The sight of blood does little to deter Golden Boy from watching me. When I have swallowed bone and fur and flesh, he clears his throat.

"I see you like the feather."

I tilt my head. "I have never seen one of its likeness before."

He smiles. "It's from a macaw. A bird found far to the south. Today, I have brought you something else."

Golden Boy reaches into a pocket. Withdraws something that flashes white, even in the dull light. He tosses it my way and I snatch it from the air without taking my eyes off him.

A neat bundle of unfamiliar material. White and stiff, the texture of a leaf with something heavier wrapped inside. I unfurl it and stare at dark lines across white pulp. Remains of a tree beaten into something flat so Golden Boy might produce an image upon the surface.

I have rarely seen my own likeness. The puddles that form from torrential summer rains have served as my only reflection. Golden Boy has gifted me with his own observations. Gangly arms and legs the texture of tree bark. Slight curves and beak-like nose, a full mane of pointed leaves covering my head and streaming down my shoulders. And of course, my vine, rooting my navel to the forest floor. There are symbols too, along with drawings of seeds. It seems Golden Boy views me as female. The classification matters little to me.

I turn to the other contents of the gift. A rock. Smooth as a vernal pool on a still day and blacker than deepest night when the moon hides her face.

"It's obsidian," he tells me. "Made by volcanos. I found it when I was traveling and thought you might like it."

I bite the stone, chip a small piece away, shudder with pleasure as it scratches down my throat. "Why have you returned?"

"Isn't it obvious? I'm curious," he says, grinning. A jay with an acorn, delighted with its prize.

"Go away, human," I say, walking as far as the umbilical cord allows. When it rains, I will suck the moisture from the earth through the vine that grounds me, taste the sweet nutrients flowing through the soil.

"May I come tomorrow? I have other such items from my travels. You seem to like them."

I do not answer, but I do not say no. For all that I would hide my own folly, I too am curious. I know nothing beyond the radius of this grove, the length of the vine extending from my middle. The world is the wall of oaks, the scream of crows. Yet Golden Boy hints at more.

When I do not answer, Golden Boy retreats. But I can tell by the jauntiness of his step that he will return again.

⸺◈⸺

Spring's first buds have blown their colors to become the greenest of leaves. And still Golden Boy comes.

With gifts and trinkets. With a smile and a laugh. With paper and pen to draw me again when I allow. And with stories.

Of white sand beaches and water that turns the color of lightning when you swim in it. Of mountain peaks swallowed by clouds. Water that carves canyons stretching towards the core of the world.

And for the first time I crave, ache for the world. For what lies beyond the stretch of a vine, the roots in the soil.

"Have you ever tried to leave?" Golden Boy asks one day.

"Of course not," I growl.

He considers me, my roots, the cord. "Would you like to?"

"No," I hiss. Remember the crashing waves he speaks of. A kaleidoscope of birds I have never seen. Reconsider. "Yes."

He grins. "I have an idea."

He dashes off and returns when the sun has reached its zenith. I have been stretching my face towards it, trying not to picture the world beyond this grove, beyond my very creation. Failing utterly. I can taste salt on my tongue, breathe desert into my lungs. I want it all and more.

Golden Boy is holding what he calls a shovel. A bit of metal and wood. Demonstrates how it might carve into the ground.

For the first time, he steps within the radius of my vine. Hesitates.

I nod, my hands down by my sides, head tilted, wondering what he will do.

When I do not attack, he smiles and approaches my root, the base of the chord that binds me to the earth. Golden Boy's face is soft, kind and sunlit as he places the point of the shovel at the base of the root.

And slices it into the ground.

I scream loud enough that each bird in the canopy takes wing, such is my agony. A heat that shoots up my roots, through my cord, sends me reeling to the ground. Electric waves radiating, pulsing. I cannot see for the pain. Can bring no end to the *thwak, thwak, thwak* of the shovel.

"It's almost—done," Golden Boy grunts.

I focus on the promise of starlit lakes. Of magma spilling from the earth. The dreams this pain will birth. Retreat deep into myself until I am a cocoon of toughest bark.

And then it is over.

Gentle hands on my roots as Golden Boy lifts them from the ground. A trophy he raises into the air. The sight of his fingers tangled in my roots is sickening.

Yet everything is new, a world of possibilities awaits.

I glance around at the grove, the only world I've ever known. The trees I have watched grow from seedlings. The crows who stand guard, always at a safe distance.

Home. But no more.

"Are you ready?" Golden Boy asks, hair dark with sweat. He tugs the cord a little, urging me forward. Into the world. Into discovery.

I take one last look at the forest. Nod.

"I'm ready for the world."

———◈———

The world is not silty sand and endless scrubland. It is a garden. Cobblestone walls covered in ivy. Manicured bushes cut to form shapes they would never take in nature. This is where Golden Boy takes me after we leave the woods.

"You still seem to be in pain," he says. "I'm going to plant you here to rest. We'll figure out a better way to transport you. And then the adventure begins!"

I nod my consent, for I am exhausted, unused to walking such a far distance. And my roots still throb. Golden Boy cut pieces of them to release the bulk from the ground, and I can feel each stump pulsate.

The pain eases when Golden Boy covers my roots in dirt once more, patting the loosened soil around my center, holding it tight.

I sit, taking in the carved shrubbery and flowers I have never seen before, flowers that must come from all over the world. Their redolent nectar washes over me as I drift in and out of consciousness, aching for the familiar scent of pine, thrumming with anticipation. The distance between my body and its forest gapes like a wound. Yet I want and want. New sights, new scents. More, more, more. I will recover. Then, I will experience everything.

While I rest, Golden Boy vanishes and returns several times, with wood, with metal, with wire. Hammer and nails.

"I'm going to build some protections for you while you rest. It will help you recover faster," he explains.

"And then you will take me to see these wonders you speak of," I murmur. My limbs are heavy with the weight of new growth, eager to replenish the damaged roots, aching to heal the pieces Golden Boy cut off so I might be free.

"Yes, of course," he says, smiling. "Rest now."

I settle into myself, into the welcoming comfort of soil. The taste is already universes different from the loamy soil of my woods. Even the small worms, the tiniest burrowing creatures, feel different.

The pain throbs, but already the sky has opened above me, the gates of the forest flung wide open. Soon I will be well again and Golden Boy will take me across the deepest oceans and into the darkest caves. I will taste the earth in each of its corners and consume it until I am sated.

I rise from my fugue to examine Golden Boy's work. He admires his own craft from afar, arms crossed, brow slick with sweat.

It is a wretched thing. Sharp angles jutting out of the ground, daggers formed from wire and metal.

"What is it?" I ask.

"Protection," Golden Boy says.

A cage, his smile reveals.

I approach, reach to the base of the cage, ready to tear it out of the ground, to free my roots.

"I wouldn't," he cautions.

When I dig my fingers into the soil, pain shoots up my limbs. I scream, yanking back my bleeding digits, horrified by the sap leaking from cuts, the burn of some chemical charring my bark.

"It's for your own good," Golden Boy says, face impassive.

"Human trickster," I hiss.

I lunge for him, thirsty for his blood. I shall bite and devour and—

My vine yanks me back, just out of reach. I shriek, the sound feral. Rabid. Useless.

Golden Boy shakes his head, ignoring my fit. "You're too special for me to traipse around the world with. But it's alright." His smile is soft, his eyes kind and bright, sparking with fever that burns away all exhaustion.

"I shall bring the world to you."

And he does.

In droves, in floods, in storms of people entering the garden walls to gawk and stare.

Once, one gets too close and I crunch her hand in my teeth, blood dripping from my mouth, bones turned to dust as I chew and she screams, clutching the stumped limb.

And still they come.

Soon, the grass beyond my range is trampled to nothing, soil compact from many feet, prying eyes, all gasping and exclaiming to see me. Golden Boy smiles at every one, talks of scientific discovery, of wonder, magic to be broken down into pieces even the least imaginative human can understand.

Each day they come. And Golden Boy has not lied. In their faces, in their languages and clothes, the world comes to me. And I rage as it closes in.

When one too many interlopers leave with missing fingers, or hair torn from their scalp, or gashes where I have struck at them, Golden Boy builds a fence. For their safety, as well as my own as he claims. Through the fence, he brings me dead rabbits and birds, uncaring that fresh blood is far more to my liking. And I eat the rotten flesh, for in this garden, the cardinals and jays will not stray. The deer know to stay safe within the forest. As I should have.

My roots accept their prison, grow downward to reach moist soil, accept that they were only ever meant to live in but one corner of the miraculous universe Golden Boy promised, never see the endless ocean nor taste prairie grass.

As my roots extend, so do my leaves, trying in vain to protect me from the relentless scorch of the sun. There is no shade in the garden.

At first, Golden Boy frets over me, fusses about with water and coverings he calls umbrellas. But his visitors complain that I am no longer free to behold.

So the umbrellas vanish. He calls my growths unbecoming. When I rest, he approaches with long sheers to clip away the leaves, until I force myself to remain awake. No matter that I ache to close my eyes in comfort. No matter that the lack of rest leaves me dull and slow. Slow enough that he may still clip a leaf here or there when he so chooses.

I scorch. I rot. I wilt. The world has become garden walls and a fence of people. A world without dreaming or sanctuary.

And Golden Boy glows in my waning light.

Even drifts of snow and biting cold do nothing to deter my visitors. I have shed my leaves, retreating into myself to survive winter's caress.

Golden Boy no longer feels the need to guide my visitors. He has returned to his adventuring. South for the season, he told me, though I did not care to hear how he would travel beyond this garden when I remained entrapped. Instead, others tell my tale to each visitor, describe my nature with a rehearsed speech, written to enthrall the most doubtful visitor.

Today, huddled amongst the masses is a woman with curling hair, shooting out in tufts from beneath a thick, green hat. I barely notice the people who crowd against the fence any longer. But something in her eyes catches me. Her scarf covers her nose, wool coat swims on her frame. But nothing can hide the eyes that blaze with a rage I have begun to ignore.

When someone elbows her, she looks away, mutters something I don't hear. She and the others in today's group leave, stomping feet, blowing on hands. She does not look back.

But the following day she returns, breath floating into the air before her as the guide gives the same speech as always. Those eyes, lit with fire, burning from the inside out, never leave mine. They burn into me even after she's gone. Still sear my chest when I hear footsteps crunching through the packed down snow after night has fallen and no one is there to observe except the waxing moon.

World painted gray, and she has dressed to match. A shadow against blankets of snow.

She places a hand on the fence and I growl, flash my sharp teeth. She keeps the hand where it is, holding my gaze, but does not come closer.

"I'm not here to hurt you," the woman says. She pulls her scarf down to reveal a wide nose and full mouth, pale skin nearly blending in with the winter's night.

I snap my teeth at her. "I tire of human lies."

She nods. "I understand. What did they promise you?"

"The world," I mutter.

Moonlit Girl sighs. "Men do like to promise that."

"And what promises are you here to break?" I ask, pacing the snowdrifts, dragging my feet through the fresh powder that fell a few hours ago.

"How are you bound here?" she replies.

I point to the cage. The awful contraption Golden Boy built. "Is it not obvious?"

"Is there more?"

"Why do you want to know?" I hiss. "Planning your own cage for me?"

She watches me, eyes beacons in the night. After a moment she speaks. "No cages. Not from me. Not ever."

"People lie. You will lie."

Moonlit Girl shakes her head. "To you? Never."

Still, I do not answer her question. Eventually, she begins to shiver from the cold, rubbing her hands for warmth. "May I return tomorrow?"

"I cannot stop you," I bark.

"No, but would you like me to?"

I consider her. The seriousness of her face, the torches of her eyes. "I do not know. But yes, you may return."

A nod. A glance to the moon crawling across the sky. She turns and vanishes into the night, leaving a torch to warm my chest.

Each night, when Moonlit Girl comes, she stands at the edge of the fence and waits for me to talk. For many nights she waits in silence until the red of dawn begins to break. When the snow begins to melt I ask her why.

"Do you want me to stop?"

"No."

A smile. Secret and small, but still there for a flash. Long enough to spread warmth from chest to root. "Because you seem lonely."

I scoff. "There are folk here every hour of the day. How could I be lonely?"

She shakes her head. "They aren't here for you though. Not really. They are here so they can tell a story that isn't their own."

"So then what are you here for?"

"To be your friend. If you'll allow."

"Hmmph."

"If you wish to talk, I would like to listen. That's why I'm here."

The sun has begun to peek above the horizon. Soon I will be surrounded by visitors once more. Moonlit Girl leaves her words hanging in the air when she vanishes.

But the next night I talk. I tell her the stories of maple leaves and wrens fussing over their nests. The freshest breath of spring and the way the stars look above a canopy. I talk, and she listens.

When I ask her story in return, it is a tale of streams and pines behind a red house in the woods. A lonely childhood and adolescence, and a never-ending journey to find the forgotten magic of the world. A love for the forest and living things that matches my own. She makes no promises, tells me no story that does not ring with truth. And one night when she sits on the fence, soaking in the spring night, I take her hand and bring her to the cage.

"The soil has something hidden in it," I explain, soaking in the warmth of her skin, feeling the balm of her touch. "Bits of metal that go deeper than the contraption you see before you. And poison of some kind, I think. I can't dig to my root, and even if I could, extracting it...hurts."

I grimace. Hurts. A small word for a universe of pain.

Moonlit Girl nods. "I have an idea. Do you trust me?"

I shake my head. "Trust is folly."

She takes my admission without complaint. "Still, I will come tomorrow."

A squeeze of my hand, and she is gone.

I do not trust, but I still count the breaths that separate me from Moonlit Girl's next appearance, devour them one by one even as strangers come to delight in my prison. Feast on them like flesh until once again she hops onto the fence. Most nights she comes empty-handed. Today she carries a worn canvas bag.

I hiss when she reaches inside, and she pauses, slows her movements, steps within range so I might easily tear out her throat if I so choose. And from her bag she pulls thick leather gloves and a heavy chunk of metal.

"It's a magnet," she explains. "To help find the bits of metal."

She pulls on the gloves and bends down with the magnet.

"No," I say, a hand on her shoulder. Gratitude and warning both. "I will unbury them myself."

After a moment's hesitation, she nods, helping me pull on the gloves, covering as much of my flesh as possible so the poison will not burn me.

"Put the magnet to the ground. When you feel a tug, or some resistance, it means there's metal."

I do as instructed, noticing the first tug with grim satisfaction.

"Here." She hands me a thin garden tool, one I have seen Golden Boy use to remove plants that he has deemed to be nothing more than weeds in his perfect garden. Time to remove weeds of my own.

The process is slow. There is far more metal than I could have imagined, and when the poisoned soil overtops my gloves, I withdraw, hissing until the pain recedes.

Moonlit Girl offers to help, but I refuse, unwilling to let another human so close to my roots again. I can see it pains her, but she stays all night long, sitting on the fence, offering words of encouragement, bits of song, shining a light on the gruesome work when even the moon hides her face in the clouds.

When the sun begins to rise, Moonlit Girl takes the discarded metal and hides it in her bag with care. I cover the holes in the bare earth.

"Tomorrow?" she asks as she does each morning when she leaves.

It is another long day of waiting. Aching for night to fall. For Moonlit Girl to return. Each night, more digging, more blades discarded, more of the trap undone. I dig and scrape, reaching ever downward, desperate for the comfort of my root, of knowing it is mine and mine alone.

Until there is no metal. Until the soil Moonlit Girl carves from the forest replaces the pieces of poisoned earth. Until there is nothing but the cage, until this too I dig free.

Moonlit Girl stands beside me, hand on my arm, my own joy alighting in her eyes.

I dig my hands into the soil, reach for my root.

Recoil back as vertigo leaves me dizzy.

Moonlit Girl crouches by my side, cups my cheek in her soft hand. "What is it?"

I shake my head. "I cannot touch my own root. And if I cannot do that, how am I meant to be free?"

"But *he* was able to do it?"

I grimace, but nod.

She rocks back on her heels and considers the disrupted ground, the cage thrown to the side.

"Tomorrow, I will bring a pack for you to carry your root in," she murmurs, eyes hard, fixed on the cage. But when she turns her head to me, her gaze is soft and full of firelight. "Will you allow me to unbury you?"

I shudder, the memory of pain shuddering acid against my skin. Soothed when she squeezes my hand.

"I will be careful," she whispers.

After a while, I nod. I cannot speak, but she accepts my answer all the same. The same way I accept the kiss she presses to my cheek.

The sky is lightening, bleeding into the new day. It pains me to replace the cage and smooth the ground about my root, but soon others will trample into the garden to gawk and stare.

Moonlit Girl turns towards the fence. Hesitates when I grasp her hand, clinging to this moment with her, the taste of freedom crackling in the air between us.

"Tonight I'll return. I promise. Do you believe me?"

The answer cloys in my throat, drowning in terror of what trust could mean. But her smile is warm. Her hand offering an escape. And I crave more of this, like a vine reaches for the sun, clawing and scraping until it has breached the canopy.

"Yes," I murmur.

She smiles. The kiss she plants on my hand warms me the whole day long. Carries me until she returns.

Moonlit Girl hops the fence with eager ease. Drops her burden and launches into my open arms. And holding her against me I feel all my breath release, the knotted coils of muscle relax. Because she returned.

She gently extracts herself from my embrace and shows me what she has brought. A bag meant to be worn upon the back, but with structure and a bed of soft soil ready to carry life.

"It will hold your root. And then you may plant it wherever you wish."

I marvel at the object, imagining how it will be to carry my root upon my own person, to be free of my tether, to have the world open before me.

A sob catches in my throat and Moonlit Girl tilts my head to hers. "Shall I begin?"

"Yes," I beg.

She kisses my forehead and moves to the root, flinging the horrid cage aside.

It is not like Golden Boy's extraction. Moonlit Girl takes her time. Digs with careful fingers, follows every pathway my root has taken so that each piece emerges intact.

The moon tracks her progress, and though I am grateful for her care, I worry about its path. For soon there will be visitors and gawkers. Soon the next marvellers will return. And I cannot wait another day for this turmoil to end. I cannot stand on the precipice of freedom for one moment longer without breathing it into my own lungs.

"Almost," she grunts, arms deep in the earth.

Footsteps drum against the ground, dreadfully familiar in cadence.

Golden Boy hops the fence without hesitation, shoves Moonlit Girl to the ground, a blade at her throat before either of us can react. A trickle of blood down her delicate neck chokes me, freezes me in place.

"Thief," Golden Boy spits. "You'll not have what's mine."

Mine. The word is poison, burning and leaching.

"No," I hiss.

Golden Boy turns to me, eyes wide with shock. "You cannot leave this place. I have kept you safe all these years. Brought the world to your doorstep."

"You lied and caged me," I growl, flashing sharp teeth. The blade does not retreat, but Golden Boy's shudder satisfies me still. "I *will* be free."

"And then what? I brought you here. Freed you from a lifetime hidden in the forest. You are nothing without me."

"I am everything without you."

I step forward, ready to claw and bite, eager for the taste of fresh flesh and blood. For Golden Boy's bones between my teeth.

But the dagger bites. More blood from Moonlit Girl, though she lies frozen, watching her captor.

"Stay here, and I shall let her go," Golden Boy says, never taking his eyes off me. "I will return the cage and the traps, but she will go free. And I will make sure you never have to see her again."

Moonlit Girl catches my eye, silently mouths, *No.*

But my shoulders droop, I lower my arms and hide my sharp teeth. Nod. "I will stay. Only let her go."

Golden Boy grins, glowing with victory. Grabs Moonlit Girl by her hair and hauls her upright, walking her to the edge of the fence, just beyond the reach of my vine, shoves her to the wooden beams.

"Leave this place, and never return," he hisses.

Moonlit Girl grunts, touches the blood trickling down her throat, and the hurt pains me as my own.

But the pain is forgotten when I grab Golden Boy by the neck and yank him back so he must stare up at me with horrified eyes.

"How—"

"You did not free me. But she did."

Golden Boy's eyes find the roots trailing across the ground, encapsulated in soil no more. Irises blue and shining.

Until I bite into his flesh, devour his screams one by one, muscle and bone recompense for the years of captivity. Chew until his bones are splinters, washed down by warm, thick blood.

When I straighten, Moonlit Girl has risen, arms slack by her sides, watching with a grim mouth.

Nothing of Golden Boy remains, for I make clean work of my meals.

"You have freed a monster," I murmur. "Do you regret it?"

She watches me a moment before retrieving the pack and carefully tucking my roots into the soft, lush soil she has prepared in the vessel. Hands me my root, my heart, and helps my arms through the straps so I might carry it across my back.

Then she faces me, hands on the straps, pulling me close so her cheek is pressed to mine.

"Never."

I sigh against her, lean into her, my own vines finding new supports. Over her shoulder, the sky is crimson gold. The sun creeps above treetops, greeted by the song of chickadees and wrens. And the horizon unfolds, endless before me.

Moonlit Girl takes my hand with a smile.

I want her. I want the world. And now, I shall have both.

Walk on Memories

Rose Regeant

RetroSPEK.

Hope flickered in Jonah's heart in tandem with the static inside his visor. The single word glimmering in the decrypted software running on his implant meant only one thing.

When he'd seen the notification for *one new message*, he'd hastily excused himself from his own engagement party, leaving behind his family and their expectations and his fiancé who was little more than a stranger.

This message was more important.

It was finally happening. After all the promises whispered through tears when they parted so long ago, vowed through the hazy interlink they only visited on sporadic occasions. Jonah was finally going to see *him* again.

He tapped his temple to shut down the decryption and erase the holographic screen floating over his eyes, revealing his lush bedroom in his parents' penthouse above a sparkling neon city. He didn't have much time. Soon, his parents would send one of the house staff to look for him. He ripped the gold band from his ring finger and tossed it onto his nightstand before plunging his hands into the soil threaded with roots that led to a pitch black stem topped with a pinwheel of cobalt petals, edges glimmering with bioluminescent brilliance. A rare Kronoan Rose in a silver planter that rested in front of his mirror. The last gift he'd gotten from the person he was about to see.

He extricated the package slowly, careful not to uproot the plants, but that wasn't easy with trembling hands. No one would ever have guessed the package he pulled from beneath the rare, sapphire flower, wrapped in plastic and marred with soil, was worth more to him than all his family's wealth.

Jonah clutched the package to his chest. Locked his door. Pulled the curtains. Didn't bother to scrub the dirt from under his nails. The AR software would paint that imperfection off him, anyway.

His heart hammered as he sat on his bed and ripped the plastic away to reveal a small, steel box, RetroSPEK etched into the metal. He knew the contents like he knew himself—the components well-organized, slotted together like a puzzle with invisible seams. Jonah had done this before, whenever *he* beckoned from across the stars. They hadn't stood in the same room in orbits, but a sim like this offered them a semblance of reunion.

When Jonah completely shut off the implant at his temple, the tech left slithered out of his synapses, leaving a silent void. He shuddered at the empty sensation. He didn't like being so alone with his own mind, but nothing could interfere with the RetroSPEK tech.

Inside the box, he found a palm-sized metal transmitter with a translucent screen and two wireless electrodes. Most intimidating of all, a syringe pre-loaded with chemical fluid that would plummet Jonah into a virtual world made of memories. Make him see everything, feel everything, as if he were actually there.

Swallowing the queasiness, Jonah unwrapped the syringe and stared at the glinting needle, the foggy fluid sloshing in the barrel. This was the part he never got used to. But the pain was worth it if they could be together again.

With a deep breath, he plunged the needle into his wrist, gritted his teeth through the agony of the drug seeping into his arm. Another jolt of pain at his temple paralyzed him. He fell back onto the pillows, breath short and rapid, until the room around him dripped into molten gold.

RetroSPEK...Loading Grid

RetroSPEK...Building Assets

RetroSPEK...Initiating SenseENHANCE

The cool touch of a breeze swept over Jonah's cheek. Wind hushed through leaves. Somewhere in the distance, water clashed with rock. His skin prickled as the numbness faded from his limbs and he groped beneath him in darkness. Smooth, malleable blades under his fingertips. Grass. And the scent of roses.

Jonah's eyes adjusted and light filtered in. He blinked a golden sky aflame with orange clouds into view. Sensation rushed into his bloodstream and he pushed himself up to take in his surroundings. Soft sheaths of grass folded over his calves, his hands pressing into the veridian pillow. Hundreds of glittering flowers bound him like a sapphire ocean. Kronoan Roses.

He reached out for one, and the petals slanted to him, drawn to his warmth. He hadn't seen so many of these since—

"Do you like it?"

The dulcet voice seeped into Jonah like melting chocolate—the same voice he'd spent too many sims burning into his gray matter. The voice he'd memorized from obsessively listening to old audio messages.

When he looked up, Chase stood in the middle of the sea of flowers. Solid. Visceral. Almost real.

Their last virtual meeting had been months ago, about two orbits after Chase had left his position as a mechanic for Jonah's family's sleek fleet of hover vehicles and space-worthy skiffs in favor of a war halfway across the galaxy. The Chase that stood before Jonah now, wading in the shimmering wild roses and bathed in the ethereal sunset, was much more of a man than he'd been when they'd fallen in love—something Jonah's family did their best to prevent because someone who worked for them wasn't worthy of their son's pedigree.

They were teenagers then—Chase gangly and awkward, too-big ears sticking out from under a bushy mop of hair he used to dye pink as he rushed around the garage with oil slicks on his overalls. Dragging Jonah up to the roof so they could search for stars in the neon-lit smog perched over their city. Talking about his plans to make the star system a better place for people like him, his family. Those who didn't enjoy the privileges Jonah had been spoon-fed since birth.

Now Chase was so much more a storm than a starry night. Tall and radiating self-assurance. Dark hair devoid of carnation hues slicked back and sealed under a black beret that matched his field jacket and cargo pants. The gun at his belt clicked as he strode through the meadow and stopped in front of Jonah to offer his hand.

Jonah took it, a jolt of warmth and electricity sparking as their fingers touched, as memory solidified their virtual contact. "I missed you," he said when Chase helped him up, hoping the sunset would drown the flush on his cheeks. Awareness of his bare feet in the grass, of his wrinkled untucked shirt, stung him. He wished he'd taken more time to get ready before uploading. Or that he'd at least remembered to update his visual preferences before loading in.

Chase held Jonah's hand to his mouth, warm lips kissing his knuckles over and over. Stopping when they brushed cool metal.

Despite the warm weather in the simulation, a rush of cold swallowed Jonah. Chase pulled away, dark eyes fixed on the gold ring around Jonah's finger.

He'd taken that off.

Chase thumbed the glinting metal. "I should have been the one to give you this."

"It wasn't my choice." Jonah cleared his throat and blinked away tears the program should have deleted. "It's just a political move. My family arranged the whole—"

"I know." Chase dropped Jonah's hand.

Jonah stared down at the ring, spinning it around his finger. Something he did often. Funny how this circle of metal that represented a link in a chain had become a source of comfort. "I took the ring off before I uploaded. I don't know why it's here. Everything else about how I look is the same as it was in real life."

"RetroSPEK is made of memories," Chase said, looking over the vast meadow of ultramarine roses. "Your subconscious built it into the sim."

"Because I was going to tell you." Jonah pressed the metal hard between his fingers, wishing the pixels would shatter between them. "My wedding is in a week."

Chase swallowed, eyes still focused on the imaginary horizon. The sunset stayed exactly as it was, the sky orange and pink. Not darkening like it would outside the sim. "Do you remember this place?"

Recall swept Jonah away in the breeze. Chase stealing one of the speeders from his parents' garage, Jonah's arms wrapped tightly around Chase's waist, out of the city to the most beautiful spot Jonah had ever seen. "Yeah, we got in huge trouble for stealing that bike and sneaking out here."

Chase chuckled. "Worth it, right?"

"Definitely." Jonah slid his hand into Chase's much larger palm. Wisps of acrid gunsmoke drifted into his nose. "This is where you first said—" He choked off his own sentence, strangled by the thick syrup of emotion and the smell of smoke that had somehow gotten stronger even though no black plumes billowed over the rose-covered hills.

He didn't need to finish because Chase knew what he meant. He squeezed Jonah's hand. "I've never stopped."

"Me either." Jonah had a feeling Chase brought him here again for the same reason—to tell him something important. Maybe it was finally time for them to be together. Maybe Chase was coming back for him for real. Jonah's heart thudded. "Why are we here now?"

Chase faced Jonah, pulling him close and grasping his delicate shoulder blades with callused hands. "Let's go somewhere else," he whispered into Jonah's hairline.

Weakness submerged Jonah as he closed his eyes and surrendered to the hold Chase had on his heart. As he buried his nose in Chase's jacket, he smelled pine. A scent so familiar, Jonah's eyes watered again. The aroma was laced with something he didn't recognize. Blood. Plasmafire. War.

The waves and wind stopped. Silence enclosed them.

Jonah opened his eyes, but over Chase's shoulder he didn't find an endless roll of flowers. Instead, he found a wall carved from polycarb and painted to look like it was made of real wood. An arched window provided a view of snow falling onto a hushed, dark forest.

A short gasp left Jonah's lips, kissing Chase's chest. "The cabin."

Chase backed away so Jonah could assess the small space, from the large (faux) wood-panel beams in the ceiling to the fire crackling in the hearth at the foot of the bed. Even their clothes had changed. Chase was no longer dressed for battle, instead barefoot and engulfed in a hoodie that drowned even his large body. Even though this memory was from years ago, the bulk of Chase's army-hardened body filled out the sweatshirt and his hair remained midnight instead of pink.

Jonah looked down at himself. Soft slippers hugged his feet and he wore the comfiest sweats he owned. He still had these clothes, shoved into the back of a drawer in the penthouse.

Jonah flopped onto the bed. "Remember how hard it was to get here? I had to tell my parents I was going to a competition with my college debate team. I actually had to join the debate team to make it sound real." He giggled into the soft down blanket as Chase reclined next to him.

"And our bus broke down halfway up the mountain," Chase recalled, folding his arms behind his head.

Jonah hummed. "Broken hoverfan."

"I had to carry both our bags the rest of the way on foot."

"And I was freezing because I didn't have a heavy enough coat." Jonah squeezed his eyes shut as they both laughed. "You gave me yours."

Something cool and soft wove between his fingers. When Jonah looked down, a pile of red and black fabric lay across his lap. A padded coat. The one Chase had stripped in the middle of an icy mountain road and draped over Jonah's shoulders before picking up both their suitcases and trudging up the incline to the cabin for their first weekend alone.

Jonah's throat clogged again. He pulled the coat over his face so Chase wouldn't see him cry. There was a reason Chase carried him back through all these memories. And it wasn't the reason Jonah longed for. Not if they were here.

"Jonah." Chase tugged the coat away and the bright snowscape streamed beneath Jonah's eyelids. Warm fingers brushed his temples. "We need to—"

"Don't." Jonah opened his eyes and shoved the coat away, sitting up and throwing a leg over Chase's hips. If Chase brought him here to break his heart again, he at least wanted to keep his white-knuckle grip on this memory as long as the sim would let him. He pressed a finger to Chase's lips. "Just be here with me."

Under Jonah's fingertip, a slow smile burned across Chase's mouth. He was so beautiful with his dark hair splayed across the blanket like oncoming night. "There's nowhere I'd rather be."

Jonah leaned forward, hands pressing into the soft mattress on either side of Chase's head, kissed his mouth, fleeting and soft. "Do you remember what we did while we were here?" It had been their first time—with the snow falling quietly and the demands of their lives locked out of their little haven.

Chase tucked his hands under Jonah's hoodie. "Yeah, I remember."

"We could do that again," Jonah said. They'd met in Retro-SPEK a few times since Chase went to war, but they'd never done this in the sim. Jonah would have liked to. A lot of people bought sim kits for virtual sex, so it wasn't taboo. But before, Jonah always felt something holding him back. Now that layer was gone, dissipated into the virtual ether just like the field of flowers Chase constructed from memory.

Chase didn't say anything. His hands crept to the hem of Jonah's cozy sweater and pulled it over his head. Jonah shivered under the touch he'd missed for so long, throwing his head back and letting Chase explore him like a star chart. Like he was a newly discovered galaxy with lightyears for the taking.

Chase rolled Jonah onto his back and stripped his hoodie. The fabric fell away, revealing a broad chest and shoulders, scarred with deep lines. Some wounds shiny and pinkish, soft with healing tissue. Others heaps of rough skin, star-shaped splatters from plasma bullets and burns like nebulae, sinuous and watercolor. Jonah didn't recognize any of them.

He touched one slash under Chase's collarbone. "What happened?"

Chase only took Jonah's hand, kissed his fingertips, pried the engagement ring off and set it on a nearby nightstand before devouring Jonah's unmarred flesh.

When they joined, Jonah crested an event horizon. A solar flare. Fiery rings pulsed and ebbed in him and he went weightless, just like he did the time Chase took him out of atmo in the beat-up spaceship he'd spent years scrounging and saving for.

"Take me somewhere," Chase murmured against Jonah's sweat-dampened skin as they hunted their breath.

"Where?" Jonah asked.

"Somewhere important to you."

"I don't know how. You always build the sim." A low sigh like a death rattle hummed around them. Out the window, a silver army-issue ship careened over the trees, smudging their perfect escape with black smoke and flame. "What—?"

"Close your eyes." Chase directed Jonah's gaze back to him with a gentle tug on his chin. "Imagine the place you want to build. Get lost in it."

Jonah didn't consciously conjure the image. The space filled him on its own, each detail a shard of shrapnel. When he opened his eyes, he was in the midst of it, standing upright, clinging to Chase. Fully dressed.

Chase kept his arms tight around Jonah's waist, fluffy hair flourishing around his big ears as he scanned the room. "My old apartment?"

Jonah backed out of the embrace and moved to the large, dirty windows that overlooked a neon-coated street. A Kronoan Rose in a silver planter rested on the sill. The air here wasn't like the fresh mountain air, or even the breeze atop the penthouse. This place smelled like stale cooking oil. Jonah gulped it in. Watched a police cruiser hover by, lights flashing and siren wailing. "My favorite place."

Chase's reflection glinted in the glass, distorted at the edges. Almost real. "Why?" His voice swept into Jonah's ear, infected with static. His hands circled Jonah's waist and he rested his chin on Jonah's shoulder. "This place is shitty."

Chase was right. This place wasn't really anything to them. Not a site of any important firsts or deep confessions. Not a monument to Jonah's heartbreak, a desolate crater in his memory. It was just a cheap studio apartment in a shit neighborhood.

And...

"The only place we were really free," Jonah whispered, twining his fingers into Chase's soft hair.

They stood in silence, like they used to, watching the passersby on the street, the steaming food carts, the brightly lit vending machines. A streak of light slashed through the smoggy sky. Then another. Another crashed into the high neck of a skyscraper, and the building bled flame and rubble and smoke.

Chase spilled soft kisses on Jonah's neck. "This is the last time I'll see you."

Jonah knew that already. Somehow, he knew even though Chase hadn't said it until now. When he'd loaded into the field of shimmering roses, he'd hoped this would mean the beginning of their real-world reunion, but somewhere in the memories they'd walked since then, he'd found Chase's true purpose.

Sleek ship like a silver knife screamed through the air and cartwheeled into the building across the street. Jonah shut his eyes before the flames reached their window. Their heat singed his cheeks, heating the scars made of tear tracks.

"I got hit on the tail fin during an in-grav raid," Chase whispered, strained and raspy. "I barely survived the crash. Pretty sure both my legs are broken. I'm not making it out of this cabin."

Jonah cleared his throat and bit down on his courage. "But you had your sim kit."

"And enough strength for one last message." As soon as Chase finished speaking, another ship swooped low, punching the asphalt below with laserfire until the street was a neat line of smoking craters.

"You could get out." Jonah spun around so their gazes met, eyes wet. "Tell me where you are, and—"

"Lightyears away." Chase smiled then. How could he smile? His thumbs ran the length of Jonah's cheeks, swiping moisture away as easily as if the tears were snowflakes around their mountain haven. "But I wanted to be here with you."

Jonah choked on his composure as the perfect future he had envisioned for them shattered like the smog-filled sky alight with a plasma-powered dogfight. Flickers of laserfire flashed on Chase's face. Jonah fought hard not to collapse, to keep this moment, this memory, corporeal for as long as he could.

"You're the only one in this whole galaxy I've ever loved," Chase said. "I wanted to—"

Jonah gasped awake in the stillness of his room. No studio apartment. No police sirens. No Chase.

As he caught his breath and oriented himself in his true surroundings, he swiped at the tears that had fallen into his hair. More nausea wracked him as he forced himself to sit up and rip the needle from his arm.

Something must have gone wrong on Chase's end. Pulled them out of the sim.

Jonah tugged the electrodes from his temples and restarted his implant, shivered as electricity crackled through his skull. He stared down at the soil lodged under his fingernails as he waited for the decryption software to boot up. At the tarnished ring lying discarded on his nightstand.

This couldn't be it. There had to be something left.

"Please," Jonah said to no one but the script running his software. A sob crept up his throat. "Please."

A soft ping flitted in Jonah's ear, signaling the decryption had loaded. A red banner flashed on his holovisor.

No new messages.

Somewhere in the penthouse, silver clinked against crystal. Voices dipped and swelled, lapping under his bedroom door like waves. A soft knock rippled from the other side of the door, each tap a ring unfurling and disturbing the surface of Jonah's grief. A gentle male voice, one he still hadn't gotten used to hearing, dropped like a stone and sank to the bottom.

This invitation wasn't a memory.

For You to Consume Me

Valo Wing

The Academy's whisper networks call Erys Roux the Prince of Devouring; warn she'll carve the name of your true love into the soft skin of your wrist with moonlit ink, promising a soulmate-level bond, only to turn around, and, with a flick of pale fingers, consume the one you desire for herself.

Well. If that's true, I want in. To be clear: not the soulmate-level-bond-to-my-nonexistent-crush thing, but the whole being-consumed-by-Erys'-fingers thing.

I mean—

Ahem.

Listen; save for the locked and forbidden door on the top floor of the eastern corridor (which frequently howls, sometimes groans, incessantly drones in the horrifying timbre of chanting monks), the Academy's tediously dull. Achingly so. Worse, per the unglamorous nature of my assignment (Project Tell No One What We're Actually Doing Here; Carry that Burden Alone), every researcher in residence—groundbreaking, award winning assholes that they are—finds it perfectly acceptable to ignore my presence.

After all, why bother with the silent shadow who's contributing nothing—okay, but I did write a book (which I then proceeded to hide deep in the library), thank you very much—when they have a heating planet to save, systems of injustice that require tearing down and rebuilding? Naïve fools, all of them.

I'd laugh if I remembered how.

But laughter is a dream from a different universe. As is escape.

I find Erys in the library. True to form, she has both legs propped on a mahogany table: ankles neatly crossed, golden Oxfords shined aggressively enough to emulate candlelight. Dusty books lie scattered about her in a casual solar storm. She's scratching thoughts into a tome with a feather quill, dress shirt sleeves rolled to the elbows. A brown curl falls over her eyes which she blows at, lazily.

It's all very extra of her. And I'm extra obsessed. (A few centuries' worth of being obsessed if my calculations of time are accurate. If accuracy is even possible in a place like this.) Anyways.

Erys chews the tip of the quill. Flips a page. She's alone, the library empty. I worry at my lower lip. Concentrate on silent inhales. Beneath my feet, a high-pitched ringing vibrates the floorboards; duets with the faint groan of the door. The cacophony morphs, crescendos, slithers Dorian mode–esque into my ears.

Warning.

I've lingered too long, spied for longer than appropriate.

Erys freezes. Tilts her head in my direction. Exhales as though annoyed and says in a voice silky as night: "Just tell me the name of the person whose heart you wish to possess, what you have to offer in exchange for my skills, and kindly slither back to your shadows, scholar."

Panic punches through my lungs. "I—uh—" Pain, agony in rusting vocal cords, unused for more centuries than I can remember.

She shuts the tome. Dust hurricanes from the pages. The title flashes, lightning-bright.

Lamentation of the Eternal: the book I wrote and hid deep in the library so the Academy's Board wouldn't find it. Hid it in hopes the right someone, someday, would pick it up, believe its pages, and prove themselves a worthy replacement for my position. I'm not allowed to outright say what's behind the forbidden door, but if someone happens upon the information indirectly...

Freedom beckons like a black hole devouring its horizon.

"Where'd you find that?" I ask, stunned. Of all the scholars here, for *Erys Roux* to find my desperate plea... "Kind of an interesting concept, wouldn't you say? The author's theory on time and—" Fuck, I'm babbling.

Floorboards murmur in agreement. A sound that burrows under my skin like the needle of a mosquito ravenous for blood. Only, I can't remember the last time I saw an insect, felt the sting of a bite the way I did on summer nights, wading in Kaaterskill creek, reflections of galaxies and moonlight shattering against my bones. Thirty-something me researching stars and immortality and horizons beyond human comprehension in my Catskill Mountain backyard.

Now there's only the Academy—its walls providing more than we could ever want or need, aren't we so lucky, so grateful—rendering the concept of *outside* laughable. Only the locked, forbidden door on the top floor of the eastern corridor and the faint hum no one questions vibrating our floorboards. Only Erys Roux and her insatiable appetite. Only the realization I *do* have something to offer the prince in exchange for a name. Because she read the book. So technically, I'm not breaking any rules. And this just might be my way out.

Desperation infuses me with manic courage. Circling Erys, I card shameless fingers through her lush curls of brown; luxuriate in the way she startles. (I'm in this now and *fuck*, it's nice being perceived.) Slide both hands over her eyes. Lean close. "The person's name I wish to possess," I say, "is Ire Darling."

She goes completely still. "But that's you."

Oh!

Her knowing my name was...unexpected; she shouldn't. No one here does—terms of my position, maintaining anonymity and such garbage *or else*. (Although why did I ever care? What did I really have to lose that I haven't already lost?) Idiot.

Erys remains unmoving, the quill frozen between fingers. "What you want isn't possible, Ire Darling."

Ire Darling.

My name on her tongue is more than I can handle. The legato drag between teeth sending shivers of star-matter down my spine. I focus on the thin veins of her eyelids pulsing a steady metronome beneath my fingers. Catch each beat between my molars, run my tongue over liquid gold, broken rules, and unquenchable need. "Are you telling me my request is too difficult?"

Erys places the book and quill on the table without removing her feet from their crossed position. Slips both long-fingered hands, nonchalant, into her trouser pockets and tips her head back; the crown of her skull brushes against my ribcage. "Your request," she drawls, "isn't *too difficult*. It's banal. Beneath me. And I'm busy."

This close she smells of ink and domination. Of places forgotten and memories warped. In the gashes where her lips have split from an abuse of worrying teeth, a glimmer of silver pools instead of blood. Side-effects of prolonged exposure to oblivion, I muse. But, *fuck it all*, I want that moonlight on my tongue, in my throat, swirling through my veins.

She chuckles: "Run along, Ire Darling. Take *Lamentation* if you'd like. I'm finding it trite."

I pull my hands from her face in a lightning flash. "You're telling me you've never wondered what's behind the door?"

There's no need to specify which, she'll know.

Erys slides both legs from the table, slamming the wooden heels of those golden shoes hard on the floor. "Nothing's behind that door."

She's not wrong.

She's also not right.

"Maybe you should read *Lamentation* again," I suggest. "Think you missed some crucial points."

A long silence embraces us.

Then—

"If I do this," she says, meditative, "you'll tell me what's behind the door."

Victory.

"Even better. I'll show you."

The violent crescendo of her insatiable hunger fills the room, cascades over ancient shelving and decrepit volumes. I cling to its feral promise, to this rush of life.

She stands in one fluid stretch of limbs. Turns her head over one shoulder, exposing the profiled bridge of her magnificent nose. "Then I suppose you have yourself a deal, Ire Darling."

Relief tingles the hollowed cavities of my bones, fills my head with a shimmer of starlight. Anticipation in all its addictive intoxication spins my brain while warning vibrations from the floor shiver my soul.

I brush past her without saying a word. (Nonchalant point goes to me!) She follows. We wind through stacks of books until reaching a quiet place; a nook I've deemed sacred, hidden from the spying and inquisitive eyes of fellow academics. A corner of refuge that's sheltered me longer than I can recall. I wrote *Lamentation* here hundreds of years ago. When I was newly appointed to my position and thought pouring loneliness into words would help alleviate the agony of learning why we were here, what it was all for. The great cosmic joke played on earth's brightest minds too preoccupied with their own goals to realize there's literally no point. That we'd been removed from the equation.

Then again, maybe my colleagues *do* realize, explaining why so many of them flock to Erys and the service she provides, hoping to find soulmates in this desolate place where nothing else matters.

However, if nothing matters, I suppose the joke is on me for my dumbass obedience to a Board that's never shown its face. I always was a sucker for rules. Damn idiot. But pointless to dwell now—

The Prince of Devouring squeezes in beside me.

And looks directly into my eyes.

Breathe, Ire. Remember to breathe. "Right," I somehow manage, all business, "how do we do this."

The corner of her mouth tilts, cocky. "Give me your hand."

Centuries since another human's said those words. So long I can't even remember: Touch-starved, desperate, and terrified, A Memoir.

When I place my palm in hers the universe slams to a screaming halt. Even the floor ceases its groaning. My body undulates in phantom-waves. Her touch is gentle but sure, soft but strong enough to bruise, and indeed I pray for those purple smudges of broken veins to mark me hers and hers always.

Studious, she flips my hand, exposing the naked want of wrist. Her brows tighten. She looks again to me and in that gaze, I taste oblivion and the velvet sweetness of night. "Ire—" She rolls my name lazily about her tongue, feigning indifference but I can sense the hesitation, the uncertainty— "are you sure?"

"Do it," I command, and she obeys.

A starlit pen appears in her hand, the point needle fine. She taps it lazily against the flat of her tongue, summoning a bead of glittering platinum. "I do this, and you'll be *yours* forever.

Severing the possibility of ever finding a home in someone else. Do you know what that means? Enduring life forever alone?"

"Do it," I repeat, firmer. Because if not this, what? If not now, when?

And she does.

Erys presses the impossibly sharp point to the skin of my wrist. Carves my name into the cells of my being. The tattoo smiles bloody in scrawling script. I count the beats of my heart around the torn edges of skin. Wait; anxious. To become hers. Hoping it's not instantaneous, that I'll have just enough time to do what's needed before vanishing.

The Prince of Devouring caps her pen, disappears it deep into a trouser pocket. Wets her lips and meets my eyes. "Well, then. The door?"

I swipe my thumb over her gift; smear red and silver in a long line down the length of my arm. Nothing's happened yet, that I can tell. Maybe it takes time, being eaten.

Groans from the door, a haunting cacophony in crescendo, *agitato*, *furioso*. A heartbeat:

Warning, warning, warning.

With a jerk of my head, I stand and lead us from the nook. She falls into step beside me, hands lost in pockets, brown curls a nebula explosion about her face. A trail of crimson-silver droplets lay bare our path for others to find. But that will be her problem—not mine—if all goes to plan.

We take to a spiral staircase, her sun-death gaze burning between my shoulder blades as we ascend and arrive on the eastern corridor's top floor. The forbidden door sits at the far end of the short, windowless hall. Cold air punctures my lungs, creeps in the crevices between stone and mortar. Behind me, Erys inhales on a sharp glissando, the Academy's rules against entering this space drilled into her very being and now at battle with her desire. But she is a knife unsheathed and ready. Godly in her insatiable need.

"Come on," I say, and she falls in line.

The door falls uncharacteristically silent—nervous as I suddenly am, perhaps, able to sense what's coming.

Erys stands beside me. Exhales with unrestrained anticipation. I race the tip of my tongue against the sharp edge of canines. Sweat beads my temple. She still hasn't taken me. And if I open that door before she's made me hers, the ramifications will be severe. I'll have broken the only rule of my position and for nothing. My earlier bravado puddles. No one's ever called me brave. I'm allowed to have doubts. Anxiety becomes my middle name. Because what if I'm wrong, what if—

"Ire?"

The cut of voice startles me. I look at her, sideways. "You knew my name, back in the library."

"Of course." She slings an arm over my shoulders, and anxiety is replaced with ecstasy incarnate. "I make it my business to know everyone here."

"But you knew it without even seeing me."

Her smirk is warm and radiant. "Divulging my methods was never part of our agreement."

Fair. It doesn't even really matter.

And yet—

I struggle to untangle the exploding mess within my chest. Tonight wasn't the first time I spied on her and we both seem to know it. "So why talk to me now? Why—"

Before me, the door; heavy with breaking silence. Behind me, a trail of blood; glittering with promise. And beside me—

A grin like desolation, like salvation. Erys speaks and the timbre is liquid with want: "Maybe I hoped you could offer something no one else could. Maybe I was waiting for the right moment."

In a thunderclap, she has my spine against the wall, her hands tight on my upper arms; pinning me in place. Erys Roux consumes the entirety of my vision, curly hair the strands of the very universe, strands of DNA; for she is both the vast largeness of the infinite and the eternal expanse of microscopic. There is no end to her, and she goes on and on forever and ever, amen.

"Take me," I beg, and her mouth meets mine.

Her mouth meets mine, and, for the first time, I understand the mysterious moon in all her kingly glory. I taste that holy light. Erys kisses me, and I ingest the dried cracks of silver spidering her lips, infusing its cosmic essence, heavy with the lives of all who have come before, into all that I am.

"The door, Ire," she reminds, urgent against my skin.

As if I'd forgotten for one moment.

We come apart and I'm struck dizzy by the rose painting her cheeks, the fire in her eyes, the heady breathlessness of her.

I slip free of her grasp. On my wrist, the name she carved has almost vanished and I know I don't have long; that it's found a new home, sunk its fangs into the soft pulp of her beating heart.

Consumption imminent. No time to waste. Freedom beckons. The whisper networks spoke true. "Give me your hand, Erys."

She obeys.

Delight and power duet through my veins. *Give me your hand.* First spoken by her, now repeated by me. I'm caught off guard by the tremble in her fingers and can't resist holding tighter. Palms joined, we go to the door. To the swirling, impenetrable wash of stone so dark it appears almost liquid. From its edges comes a droning, barely there, but undeniable.

I'm ready.

(Kaaterskill Falls and stars in churning midnight waters, dream-bright dancing over skin. Mosquitos and blood and too many nights suffocating under academic papers, hands cramping as I composed my thesis. Honeysuckle in the air. The beating pulse of a passing plane cutting through smog-hazed skies.)

Does any of it still exist beyond my memory?

Or is memory enough to keep a world alive, real.

Her grip in mine clenches. "Ire—?" Light panic threads her voice.

I exhale, hard. It doesn't matter what's happening back home. Realistically, it's all dead anyways: the mosquitos and the stars, the water poisoned beyond imagination.

"Ire. The door."

Right.

There's no handle. No knob. No way in. No way out. I run five fingers across the shivering stone. It knows me on a cellular level. Responds. Side by side with the woman I've worshipped for a quiet century or more, what was once door melts into crystal-cut glass.

And reveals the endless stretch of the universe.

Erys jerks backward. "*No.*"

"I'm afraid so," I confess, almost regretful, remembering the horrible day I learned the truth as well, the great trick that'd been played, and *oh* if only I could burn the Academy's acceptance letter, if only I drowned it in the creek along with my egotistical dreams and just *stayed home* where maybe I could have made a real difference.

"But we're on earth, we're academics on sabbatical, we're—"

"In a space station on the horizon of a black hole."

"*No,*" weakly repeated, nothing more than a whimpered gasp.

I maneuver myself to stand behind her, resting my chin on one shoulder, inhaling the sweet inky musk of her curls. Small human moments for a few precious minutes more. I've had so few in this long-suffering, lonely life. Time barely exists on a black hole horizon, or, at least, exists at a rate so slow it practically doesn't.

"Immortal," I spit. "That's what we are. Impossible and trapped and nothing more than specimens under the guise of earth's most prestigious minds granted the honor of a life-long sabbatical. How stupid we were. How easy we made it for those threatened by our research to remove us from the equation entirely."

The press of her body against mine is fire. The glass window before us, ice. An expanse of beautiful dark stretching fingers, begging us to leave this place behind, to join its holy song. "This is your burden to bear now, Erys. My time is done."

A hard light eats the cold black of her pupils. "Why me, Ire?"

The name on my arm vanishes, my life-force bleeding into her.

I take her face in my hands. Say with fading breath: "Because, Prince—" A smile, vicious and tender as space— "if anyone can devour a black hole, if anyone can find a way out of this and end the experiment, save us all—it's you."

Her pupils dilate, swelling black, black, black as space. She's afraid but knows I'm right. Erys Roux can accomplish that which I couldn't, and I believe this with all that I am, all I know to be true, my eternal benediction: Erys Roux, Erys Roux, Erys Roux.

"Why now?" Her voice, ragged, desperate almost.

I shrug, unable to resist throwing her words back at her, her face so delicate in my hands, so precious; the best weapon against our situation I could find. "Maybe I was waiting for the right moment."

"For?"

I laugh. One last exhale, and I'm free.

"You to consume me."

THE ABERRANT SEA
ALISTAIR REEVES

CONTENT WARNINGS: MILD TRANSPHOBIA

The village of Duncaster rotted in the bay, changing in spite of all its stubborn attempts not to.

It clung to the shale rocks, the wharf's fingers clutching shore to prevent the whole place drowning. Salt-bleached houses lined the cliffs like yellowed teeth. Its obstinate people were mostly born and buried there, in the rocky soil and salty winds where nothing much could grow. The waters, however, were full of fish.

Avery Dunnett stood ankle deep in a pile of herring on the deck of her tiny trawler, Prophesea, when she spotted something yellow amongst the writhing silver. The fish gasped like all fish-out-of-water do, but this one had a seam opening it like a purse from throat to tail. Its acid yellow insides crawled slowly out of the seam. It wasn't the first aberration. Only yesterday she'd found a fish with eyes bubbling like roe along its scales.

This new monster, unzipping its skin like a jacket, gave her a stab of envy. How nice it would be to take off her own skin for a day.

She took it by the tail and smacked its head off the gunwale, but it arced around and sunk its teeth into her wrist. Hissing, she hit it again. It went limp, and she wrapped it in a plastic bag kept for such occasions as these. She'd seen a few other fish like it. None had bit her. Whatever disease it had, she hoped it wasn't catching.

Rain boiled the sea when Prophesea trundled reluctantly to berth. Avery tucked her plait into her soaked cap and carried the crates of herring to market two at a time. She passed faces as familiar and repetitive as the mooring cleats interspersed along the wharf. The Murphy sons unloaded crab pots and gave her their customary nod. Penelope Baker came smelling like sweet pea, delivering a berry tart baked for Sean Finnigan, whom she'd surely marry before spring turned summer. Timothy Dowling waited at the end of the pier to heckle Avery for looking like a boy.

Timothy had the face of a monkfish yet none of its flavour. Why he should be upset that *she* was ugly, Avery would never know.

After hauling her catch to the fishmonger's, she went home, where her father was upholstered in his usual armchair. She made trout soup and set it on the tv tray in front of him. He leaned forward, rubbing his leg. An accident during a storm had broken it years ago—he'd just come to berth, and the waves rocked him overboard. His leg had been crushed between Prophesea's hull and a pier support. He'd never fished again, and treated that like a castration. The sweet father Avery knew soured into a stranger who viewed her competence as a theft.

She warmed her hands on her bowl and half-watched the grainy television.

"Emmett Kincaid came 'round again," said her father.

She braced herself. "How's he?"

"He asked my permission to marry you again."

"And you told him I wasn't interested, didn't you?"

"You can't stay a spinster forever."

"I can."

His spoon clattered in the bowl, watering the tv tray with broth. "Ave, I don't want to be a tyrant 'bout it, but I can't keep you here."

Avery put her own soup down, uneaten. "Why not?"

"Because it's not how it's done, you taking care of me. Emmett's a nice man, a good man, and he's loved you since you were small. There's no one better for you, not in Duncaster, and—" He paused, lips flapping around the words. "With Emmett, you'll be fine. Just 'cause I'm sinking don't mean you have to go down with your old man's ship."

Avery swallowed thickly. "I could get another job."

He slammed his fist on the table tray. "Ave, I'm not askin', I'm telling you. You're marrying that man."

Her heart felt pinched in a crab claw. There wasn't anything wrong with Emmett Kincaid. He was nice-looking by Duncaster standards, meaning all his features were more-or-less symmetrical, and he washed well. He treated her kindly. She could fault him for nothing.

Except.

When he looked at her he saw the chitinous shell. He would find the open, filleted version unappealing in a wedding gown or warming his bed. She knew he loved the costume of her flesh more than the heart of her.

"I'll wash up," she said.

By morning, Avery woke with a sore wrist. She removed the bandages she'd applied last night. Beneath, the bite wound festered brown with a pattern like scales up her thumb and wrist. Her alarm at the sight felt dull. It tapped her mind from behind aquarium glass, the place she kept all feelings too uncomfortable to submerge herself in. Somehow, her body changing alarmed her less than the idea of marrying Emmett Kincaid.

She washed the bite. Then she put gloves over it, because what else could she do? Tell the town doctor? He'd amputated limbs for less alarming infections. She'd figure out what to do later.

Her boat, the sea, and Duncaster greeted her with the same words as they had every day for as long as she could remember, until she took her catch to the fishmongers.

A man with a pearl-drop earring stood outside. He wore a scarf the colour of fresh lemons and, in spite of the rain, held no umbrella. His hair painted his forehead in squid ink swirls, and when he saw Avery he smiled brighter than any lighthouse.

"Just the man I was waiting to meet," he said.

Unlike when Timothy Dowling said she looked like a boy, this man made it sound sweet to Avery's ears. She didn't correct him.

"Me?" she said.

"You fish around these parts, don't you?"

"Yes."

"Then let me introduce myself." He gestured to himself with a flourish. "My name's Zuhair. If you don't mind my asking, have you caught anything strange in these waters from time to time?"

Avery hadn't spoken to anyone about the aberrant fish. The people of Duncaster liked things just so and viewed anything different as a nuisance or worse. From their sideways looks, they saw Zuhair—brown-skinned and eccentrically dressed—the same way. But he struck a strange affinity in her which made it hard not to indulge her curiosity.

"Strange in what way?" she asked.

"Not unnatural per se, because I theorise these things happen naturally. It is nature, after all. Perhaps metamorphosed? Transformed. Have you seen any fish like that?"

Because he'd asked so nicely, and because she didn't want to give him the occasion to say 'goodbye,' she said, "Come with me."

He looked out of place—a cheerfully prismatic paint smear on the overcast canvas of Prophesea's hungry, anaemic deck. She took up the plastic bag with the strange herring and showed him.

He peeled open the bag and held the fish with delicate respect. Avery felt a sudden twinge of guilt for killing it. With a thumb, he opened the seam of its belly. The luminous guts nearly slipped out, dissolved and strange in consistency. Before their eyes, the innards moved, wrapping around the fish like a shawl, and it shot from his hands. It flopped once, slimed across the deck using its veil of viscera as limbs, then returned to the sea over the gunwale's lip. They both watched it vanish into the dark water like a falling star.

Zuhair said, "I thought so."

Avery found his response strange and liked it. "What?"

"How many fish like this do you catch?"

"Used to be one a month, maybe. Now one or two a week?"

"Were any like that one?"

"No two alike, to my eyes."

"I've found the same." His finger formed a fish hook, which he tapped against his chin thoughtfully. Avery swallowed a stone of envy watching the thick bones of his hands, the snaking purple veins.

"What's happening to them?" she asked. "The fish."

"They're changing, though I don't know how or why." He animated with enthusiasm as if reeling in an idea. "Would you help me? You could sail us around the archipelago. We'll fish for the changelings until we find where their population's densest."

"Why? Are you a marine biologist or—?"

"Not as such. Let's just say it's of personal interest. So how about it?"

"I—" Avery hesitated.

Looking at his fancy clothes, she couldn't imagine Zuhair thriving on her damp, old boat. This wasn't what bothered her, though. It wasn't the length of the voyage, either. She'd gone on a few when the catch in their bay thinned out. She'd only had cause to drop anchor and sleep in the cramped cabin a countable number of times, but provided the weather was good, they'd be fine. It wasn't even that she mistrusted him. The townsfolk mistrusted outsiders, but she had always felt like one, so it made her feel kinship to him.

No, it wasn't these things which gave her pause. Intuitively, she sensed an adventure with Zuhair would crack open the aquarium where she kept all the secret parts of her Duncaster could never swallow. She'd return sea-toughened, marinated in salt and cured into something the brittle town could not withstand.

Her wrist throbbed. She imagined Emmett Kincaid waiting at an altar, and her insides felt like the herring's looked.

Zuhair said, "I can give you time to think about it—"

"No. I'll do it."

She packed clothes for a week at least. Soap, tinned food and jerky. She contemplated space and whether it was too indulgent to include a packet of liquorice candies.

Not if she ate them on the way.

She told her father she needed to fish beyond the bay and might be away for a few days, then went to find Zuhair.

He waited on the wharf, speaking to Phillip Murphy and holding a crate of clothes. Zuhair's lighthouse smile failed to brighten Phillip's frown.

"Ah, there she is," said Phillip. Avery's heart flipped into her throat. Zuhair thought she was a man, and Phillip had spoiled it with a single syllable. She hadn't realised how much she preferred the ruse to reality until it was taken.

Zuhair blinked. Like a camera shutter taking a new picture of her. He didn't comment, though. "Phillip here was just warning us against our adventure."

"I've seen them mutants. You're mad to go searching them out."

"You're not the first to say so," Zuhair replied. "But Avery's very capable. I'm in good hands."

"I'm more worried about her in yours," Phillip said. "Avery, listen here. You're a good girl. Known you since you couldn't walk or talk. Mark me, this man means trouble."

Avery steeled herself. "A little trouble never hurt now and again."

Phillip looked pointedly at Zuhair. "Emmett will worry."

She ignored the implication. "They're just fish. How bad could it be?"

Her wrist itched, but it didn't matter. She'd made her decision.

Once Phillip stormed off, Zuhair said, "I don't think he likes me."

"You're not from here. Liquorice?"

"I thought I was the only one who liked these. I knew we'd get along. So."

He looked askance, oddly shy. Tension twitched like a bitten fishing line between them. She helped him heave the crate of clothes on board. She'd never have let him have so many on a ship tight for space, but he was handsome. Once loaded up, he revealed the source of his anxiety.

"Phillip called you a 'she.' I'm sorry. Should I have done the same?"

Avery startled. No one had ever asked. Did she get to choose?

If she prised apart the chitinous shell Emmett Kincaid thought he loved, there was a boy. She rarely looked at him directly. At thirteen his body betrayed him. It bled and grew lumps where he didn't want them. The boys he used to play games with stopped inviting him or tried to kiss him. He'd lost his friends and an enigmatic something—deep-sea strange and hard to understand.

"No," Avery said. She—no, *he*—rolled the liquorice around his mouth. "You had it right the first time."

Prophesea chugged out of the uncomfortable crescent bay, sailing towards a shoal of islands spattered across the Eastern coast. Avery dropped the trawl net and watched Zuhair from the wheelhouse. He stood at the bow, looking out to sea, then glanced over his shoulder and smiled.

Something about him unnerved and entranced Avery, drew him in and upset the delicate compromise he'd made with himself years ago. If Duncaster was a prison, and Avery had spent years making it as comfortable a home as jails could get, it seemed Zuhair had stuck a key in his locked cell and left it there.

They recalled the trawl net before twilight stole the day. The aft heaved with fish. Mostly mackerel, but something larger thrashed and snapped a meal out of its fellows.

It was once a yellowfin tuna—a sizeable four-footer. The tuna's mouth extended longer than the usual pout, cleaved open to the gill to accommodate teeth like porcupine quills, bits of mackerel caught between. The serrated spine of the creature usually summoned images of saws and bread knives, but this one's ventral and dorsal fins had grown the length of scythes. They cleaved through the shoal and tore holes in the net. Its eyes had grown to squid-sized proportions, so bulbous they nearly touched on the top of its head.

"This one's going to be tricky to examine," said Zuhair, eyeing the spikes.

Abruptly, the pile of mackerel seethed like boiling water. Their silver-blue bodies flipped and gaped and turned on the tuna. Little mouths took dime-sized bites out of the larger fish's flanks. Avery cried out in alarm. Unthinking, he seized the tuna by the tail and dragged it from the net. Mackerel stuck to it like leeches. Zuhair, mincing around the flailing fins, plucked them off, but it was too late. The half-eaten tuna's gills ceased flaring for oxygen.

It wouldn't have lasted long out of water, and Avery didn't have a tank for it, but it felt a shame anyway.

They shovelled the treacherous mackerel back into the sea before squatting down to examine what was left of the tuna. There wasn't much, but the eyes still rolled reflexively. Avery wondered if it had a mind equally large to comprehend what was happening to it.

"Why do you think they're changing like this?" Avery asked while Zuhair poked through the fish's insides.

"It's hard to say. Normally, evolution is driven by natural selection. New dangers or environmental changes require new defence mechanisms and adaptations. The fish with them survive, those without don't and can't pass their genetics on. This tuna has plenty of new adaptations."

"So it could be there's a new predator?" That was alarming, given the tuna's only natural predators were things large and dangerous as sharks, sea lions, orcas.

"Could be. But evolution normally takes tens to hundreds of thousands of years. These fish are changing before our eyes."

Avery chewed his lip, thinking about the boy he'd become the second Zuhair gave him the option to call himself one. It wasn't the same, but— "Could it be the opposite?"

"Hm?"

"You said normally it can be driven by dangers or environmental changes, but can it go the other way? When the world is a little safer, do they become more—themselves? Less afraid, even if that version of them is more frightening."

Zuhair tapped the hook of a finger to his chin once more, a gesture that made embers glow in the coal of Avery's heart. What if he took that hand and curled their fingers together?

"Yes, it works that way, too. There was a bird which evolved flightlessness on an island without ground predators, but went extinct during a flood. A cousin species migrated back to the very same island and evolved flightlessness once more. Everything can change one way or another, all the time. But this—" He pried open a flap of glass ribs to show the heart of the tuna throbbing inside. "This is something else. ACK—"

Whether a reflex or not quite dead, the tuna flailed. The scythe of a fin caught Zuhair as he reeled back, slicing open his shirt. He stumbled, grasping at his bare chest. Avery's panic turned to confusion. He thought the tuna had scored Zuhair open, but the marks on his chest were old. Two scars ran under his pectorals, nearly meeting in the middle and darker brown than the rest of his skin. The sight felt like split glass. The aquarium inside Avery spidered with cracks but held together. Just.

"Are you all right?" he asked.

"I liked this shirt," Zuhair answered.

It felt rude to push for more, so Avery didn't. They stowed the tuna's questionably dead remains in the hold as a temporary measure until they knew what to do with it.

The sun's light failed at the rim of the world, so it was time to drop anchor and turn in. They ate tinned beans, hardtack and cured meats by companionable candlelight, during which Avery made no attempt to keep his sleeve from rucking up where scales would show. He wanted Zuhair to ask. To know. He felt sure Zuhair saw, but they went to bed without commenting on one another's scales or scars.

Over the next three days, they fished and found all manner of strangeness. Jellyfish with bioluminescent glass eyes in their domes. A spiny seahorse with metallic plating. Something they could barely identify which turned out to be a stingray's skeleton but inexplicably alive.

Avery didn't know if they were any closer to answers, and found he didn't want any. He just wished to spend more days exploring these impossibilities with Zuhair, whose non-judgmental exploration made Avery brave enough to pick at his own insides.

On the fourth night, Avery woke. The clock's red glow read five past three in the morning. Waves licked the hull and rain drummed its fingers on the deck. Normally the sea's music would calm him, but Zuhair's sleeping bag lay like a deflated shark's egg, empty. Avery called his name but got no answer.

He took a torch. The claustrophobic beam illuminated the clutter, but everything around its light fell to pitch. A lot of things could hide so long as they dodged out of the questing beam.

He shuddered and headed toward the door. Then he heard it.

Something clambered wetly up the starboard hull. The whole boat canted under the weight of it hefting itself aboard. Avery stumbled as the ship overbalanced in the other direction. He fell into the stairs, landing on something soft. With a slick shiver of horror, he recognized Zuhair's clothes.

On deck, something moved. It didn't step. It dripped and slapped. From the stairs, Avery could see light playing under the crack of the door. A shadow moved. An eerie voice haunted its way into his head. It sounded like whale song and the resonant glide of a finger over a crystal glass's rim, sweetly threatening.

Whatever it was, Zuhair was up there with the thing, inexplicably naked or drowned already. A shock of anguish crushed Avery's chest. Not because they'd known each other long, but because they hadn't had the chance to.

With a burst of rage or bravery— he didn't know which—Avery slammed through the door, twisting the torch around until it fell on something draped across the deck. Scales the colour of oil slick. Folds of black flesh—an eel's tail. His torch drifted up metres of length, its loops and coils and veiling fins like poorly stowed tackle wrecked across the deck. The beam of light came to the creature attached.

It perched on the stern. It had its back to him. A back that could pass for human if not for the gills slitting its ribs and that never-ending tail in place of legs. Its inky hair was soaked to the skull. It could breathe out of water, because its ribs inflated like bellows, each notch of spine countable.

The horror in Avery's heart stilled under a caress of intuition. Looking at the creature, he stopped feeling afraid and felt yearning instead. This was not human. It was not fish. It was its own thing. It sang again, and this time Avery's body was a tuning fork. Resonating, mirroring the song. Like to like.

"Hello?" he said.

The creature jerked around. In the torchlight, its eyes flashed like round coins.

It dove. The folded length of tail let out like a line hooked on a big catch, zipping over the gunwale. Avery ran in time to see the splash. Gone.

His wrist pained him so suddenly, he nearly dropped the torch. Hissing, he pulled back his sleeve.

The infection had spread. The bite itself looked healed, but the skin surrounding it was mottled with scales up to his elbow. His hand stiffened into a claw, and for a second, when he formed a fist and then stretched his fingers, it looked as though a membrane connected them before sucking back into the skin.

Breathing hard, he went to the cabin. He nearly tripped on the clothes. Picking them up, he examined them more closely in the torchlight. No blood, no tears. Nothing to indicate Zuhair had been violently wrestled from his bed.

The alarm Avery should have felt when he first laid eyes on his festering bite wound finally leaked through the cracked glass where he'd kept it. Was that creature the thing he would become if the infection wasn't cut from his arm? What should he do now that Zuhair was gone? Just as he'd feared, Duncaster felt cut off to him. They would not welcome someone half-fish. He'd spent years on the open ocean and only now understood what people meant when they said they felt lost at sea.

He stayed awake in his bunk through the night, watching in the dying light of the torch as new scales split his skin and the membrane sloughed away. He tied a tourniquet around his arm. He thought about amputating it, but he didn't have the tools and besides, of the parts of him he wanted removed, his arm never made the list.

The boat rocked. Something clambered up the hull once more. This time, Avery didn't hesitate to run up to the deck. He had little left to lose.

But he didn't find the monster. He found Zuhair, naked and soaked in ectoplasmic ooze. His sunrise-gilded shoulders heaved, and in dawn's light his body challenged and enchanted Avery's imagination.

They had the same parts.

With a shock of realisation, Avery understood the monster and the man before him were also the same. He felt the way cracking glass sounded, creaking under the enormity of what he could no longer contain.

Zuhair shivered, propping himself up on an elbow and giving a rueful laugh. "I don't suppose I can bother you to get me a towel and some clothes?"

While he dried off and made himself decent, Avery boiled water for tea, watching dried leaves swell into slimy mulch and wondering what had become of Zuhair's fish tail. Did it shed away like a snake's skin, break off like a gecko's and grow legs? Or did it just dissolve into mist? Had he dispensed with breasts in the same way, leaving only scars behind? What world had he come from, for the flat triangle of fur between his legs to make him feel no less a man?

Pouring cups, Avery trembled enough to spatter himself. Twenty-nine years and his youth spent on a body that never belonged to him. Wasting away in the carapace of womanhood when there'd been other avenues. Monkfish-faced Timothy Dowling hurling insults that landed in sore places, but not the kind he'd aimed for. Emmett Kincaid in love with an imaginary girl. And worst of all, Avery's father, who'd known and taught Avery to fish and let him wear boy's clothes, but wouldn't let him cut his hair or refuse a proposal.

They took their tea in the wheelhouse. Zuhair came dressed in tight trousers and a loose shirt open to the navel, no longer hiding his scars, and the suffering built up in Avery's heart had no place else to go. The aquarium containing it was in pieces, and Avery was soaked in feeling.

"Were you ever going to tell me?"

Zuhair paused, taken aback by his tone. "Well, I wouldn't have kept it secret forever, but it's hard to tell someone I'd just met, 'I think I might be turning into a fish.' So—"

"Not that." Avery pointed to his chest. Somehow, Zuhair being half-fish wasn't what made him feel betrayed. "You. You're— like me. You knew."

"I suspected," Zuhair acknowledged.

"But you didn't say anything. You could have—" What? Avery didn't rightly know what Zuhair could have said. If the information could be called a secret, he hadn't held onto it for long.

"This is...delicate. Were you going to drink that?" Zuhair said.

He took his cup of tea and ran a finger up the spoke of Prophesea's wheel, taking his time to answer.

"It's not easy telling people who I am. They don't always take it well."

"But we're—"

"Alike. I thought so, too. Call it kinship, maybe. But I didn't know whether that sense came from who we are or what we were becoming."

Avery grasped his wrist reflexively, though the scales had spread past his elbow now, a few speckling the back of his hand.

"Either way," Zuhair finished, "it wasn't my place to tell you who you are, and I won't apologise for waiting to tell you who I am. But...I'm sorry the world wasn't more forthcoming that people like us exist."

Before Avery could answer, Prophesea keened like a wild hart, an inhuman sound of creaking wood. Alarmed, they fled the wheelhouse to search out the source. They found the deck buckled and warped. Worse, sounds issued from the hold, gurgling and gnashing. Avery summoned enough gumption to fling the hold's hatch open.

He took an involuntary step back. The aberrant tuna was no more. In its place, the belly of the hold was an open mouth with teeth packed together like baleen. They chewed and yawned, sucking the crumbling innards of the boat into itself. The hull made the noises of polar ice shifting. Mournful groans and snaps. Wood splintered, and the maw grew, as if it could devour itself and Prophesea whole. Water should have spewed forth from its gullet, but all Avery could make out was the wet squelch of a muscular throat lined with more teeth.

Zuhair said, "It appears your boat wants to be something other than a boat."

Fear lanced through Avery. If Prophesea continued this way, would it devour itself and its sailors? He didn't want to wait to find out.

Dashing back to the wheelhouse, he set a course for the closest island—a mere freckle of stone in the sloshing sea. It wasn't far, but Avery knew better than most that it was easiest to shipwreck in the shallows than out in open water. He hoped the monstrous belly of the ship wouldn't prevent them from reaching safety.

Zuhair joined him. "Where are we off to?"

"Land."

Zuhair didn't look half as panicked as he should have, but then he could breathe underwater just fine. Easy for him. Avery's transformation was far from complete. He'd gotten to spend four blissful, salt-spray days as a boy, and now— He scrubbed at his hands, at the truncated spread of scales. Zuhair's soft face crumpled with concern.

"You don't want to change?"

"I did. Do. Not like this."

"Then how?"

Avery didn't know how to articulate it. "I just wish I'd had more time."

"What do you mean?"

"I wanted to be a boy, not a monster."

Zuhair looked wounded. "Is that what you think we are?"

"Not you, I—"

"We're changing," Zuhair said. "It can be frightening, but is it any scarier than staying the same?" Soft, gentle as he'd held the mutant herring, Zuhair touched Avery's cheek. "Monsters get to be all the things no one else is allowed. It's kind of freeing, if you think about it. You can be a boy, too. You can be both."

Fearful desire singed a cigarette burn into the centre of Avery's heart, because between this world and all the unknown ones, he'd never wanted anything more, but somehow wanting and taking felt like different things. Wanting it was a comfortably familiar suffering, and taking it felt futureless. Where could he go if he became a stone Duncaster couldn't swallow? The only place he'd called home would turn inhospitable.

The boat heaved. Avery lost balance, careening into the wall. Regaining his legs, he took the wheel, trying to right their course to cut through the surf, but Prophesea had a mind of her own. She pulled to port, beam to swell. Avery heaved on the wheel, but it would no longer obey his whim. A ferocious enough wave could capsize them like this.

Holding the rail down the steps with an iron grip, he went to investigate the problem and found the mouth surging up out of the hold, chewing on the edge of the open hatch. Inside, stretchy flesh was punctured by an eye, searching for escape. Prophesea was turning herself inside out, and the newly asymmetrical, meaty weight of her pulled the entire boat portside, threatening to pour them out into the sea.

Avery looked out at the island he'd aimed for. Still a long distance off, but swimming had become safer than sailing. As if reading his intent, Zuhair took Avery's hand. He tried to lace their fingers but couldn't. They had webbing in between each one.

"It'll be all right. I'm a strong swimmer," Zuhair said.

Prophesea lurched. Before Avery could change his mind, he jumped and launched them into the ocean.

At the same time, Prophesea's mouth snapped free, dragging its hull inside out, planks of wood layered like armoured plates. She surged into the air like a breaching whale then dove for the deep. The vestigial limb of her boom cut through the water and caught Avery in the ribs.

He thought he felt them crack. His hand wrenched painfully from Zuhair's grasp. In the black water with salt in his eyes, Avery couldn't see, only knew from the pop of his ears that he was sinking.

Prophesea descended at speed, the pressure of water against Avery's back keeping his stomach pinned to the boom. His old boat dragged him down.

The deep breath he'd held burst out of him in a stream of bubbles. His lungs compressed around the vacuum of air and pressure.

The futility of escape left no room for anything but thought, and the first one kissed his mind with deep irony. Only a few minutes ago, he'd mourned the boy he'd never gotten to be, and the monster he would become. He'd felt futureless, unmoored from the only designs life had for him before he set sail with Zuhair. Now, while death dragged at his harrowed lungs, it seemed foolish to have feared a future of monstrousness over allowing his soul to gather dust in Duncaster.

Darkness closed in. The light of the surface twinkled like an aurora. A darting shape blotted it temporarily, a haunting song drifting down. The shape reappeared. It swam towards him. He recognized the sinuous length of tail and iridescent scales.

Zuhair took Avery's face in hand, his song an aura around him. Somehow Avery knew what it meant.

Breathe.

How? The sea was breathless as deep space.

Zuhair's brow folded. He closed eyes that saw Avery plain and unshelled. He leaned in. Avery's failing heart leapt at the press of lips pushing a breath of water into his mouth. Water, not oxygen. Zuhair pulled back, and more water rushed in, filling Avery's lungs, threatening to burst him open, except—

He drew a new sort of breath, cold and fresh. The pressure receded. The encroaching darkness in his vision faded. Gills opened like vents under his chest, his ribs. His shirt sucked into them, so he struggled out of it. Trousers, too. The rest of the change ripped through him, painful like peeling his skin off hot leather in summer. But there was relief in it, too, as his body flattened. Moulted. The scales patterning his arms consumed the rest of him, legs melting together. He shed his skin and slipped free of the boom in one powerful flick of his new body. Prophesea streamed past them, twisting into the deep.

Zuhair beheld him. Avery was afraid to look, too. When he did, he expected joy, fear, anxiety, something big and jittery.

He looked and felt calm as a cloudless sky. Like a hermit crab that had shucked one poorly fitting shell for another, and found it cosy enough to call 'home.'

He sucked it in. New breath, new body, and a serenity so buoyant it nearly floated him to the surface.

———◈———

The sea rose to Duncaster's shoulders, threatening to swallow it. Avery's father braved the wind and his bad leg to walk along the pier. He came to the empty dock cleat where Prophesea once moored.

His daughter had not and would never return, but a son waited on the edge of the pier, his tail draping into the water like the only dress that ever fit him.

"What happened to you?" said his father, horrified.

Somehow Avery knew it had less to do with the tail and more to do with his lack of breasts, with the new tenor of his voice—tinny and inhuman but distinctly lacking a girlish chime.

He responded simply, "I changed."

His father's expression curled like a fist, tense with uncertainty. He looked more like a lost boy than Avery had ever felt, and in that moment he pitied him. What a dead end manhood had been if an injured leg was all it took to strip him of it. The angry coals of Avery's heart cooled. His stiff, defensive expression softened. Wordlessly, he held out a hand, inviting his father to sit with him on the pier like they used to. Once a fragile father with his futureless daughter, now—maybe, hopefully—father and son. Just that.

His father turned to stalk away. The immediate sting of it nearly sent Avery splashing back into the sea, but he paused. A lesson his father imparted on fishing came to him. You couldn't always fight. Sometimes you had to let the fish take the line out. If Avery let him exhaust his anger, maybe they could be reeled back together.

He watched his father limp to a stop. His shoulders sloped. He turned.

He needed Avery's hand to help him sit. Painstakingly, he did. With a sigh of release, he said,

"Well, you won't have to marry Emmett Kincaid."

FLICKER, BEAT, SPARK
TALIA GREER

CONTENT WARNINGS: GRIEF, DEATH

The tag of Natalia's new black dress scratched the back of her neck as she sat onstage and stared into the darkness of the open-air auditorium. Nighttime heat pressed in, almost suffocating in its persistence, and the energy of the community—everyone packed into their only gathering space for the funeral—was a somber hum. Countless pairs of eyes pierced through the black to settle on her and the rest of the orchestra, an eerie one-way mirror.

Her hand trembled once above the strings of her cello. In response, she schooled her entire body to stillness and glued her eyes to her father, the conductor. There was a pause as he swept his eyes over the waiting musicians. Then, his hands began to move. Natalia's skin rose into gooseflesh as he beckoned first to the pianist and then gently, expertly, brought in the flutes.

The music rose and fell, wrapping her in its embrace and sweeping her along for the ride. It was a delicate medley of Victor's favorite songs, she'd been told. Easy pieces. No dancing today, and certainly no magic. All she had to do was wear her dress, look pretty, and play along.

As the cellos tiptoed in, low and sweet, she realized she was proud of herself. She'd expected the funeral to be much worse—*herself* to be much worse—and it was a pleasant surprise to continually find herself upright and playing her cello. She could do this. Just this medley, the ceremony, and a short piece in closing, and she could wipe her hands of the whole sticky ordeal.

The violins bowed out. The rhythm slowed, gentle pushes from the flutes moving things along. Natalia flipped to the next page of music and began to play. It took her brain a moment to catch up to the tune: the high, keening violins, and the cheery darkness of cellos cupping them from underneath. Her breath caught in her throat.

No.

They wouldn't. They wouldn't do that to her.

But it was his favorite song. Of course they would.

She'd been practicing the wrong sheet music. Somewhere along the line, the medley had been changed, and she'd been left out of the loop. Fortunately, though, or perhaps not, she still knew this song by heart.

Natalia's finger slipped. The oboe covered her mistake, so she kept playing, but she was shaking now, all over. She closed her eyes. Notes came to her automatically, the result of numerous afternoons spent in the ballet studio, bent lovingly over her cello as Victor twirled across the floor. It was *their* song. So undeniably Victor and Natalia that none of the other pairs dared to play it. Here, it was just a sampling folded into the greater medley, but that was enough.

Memories flickered across the movie screen of her closed eyelids. First it was Victor's mouth, wide open in a laugh, then his body, muscles taut and rippling beneath sun-kissed skin as he arched up and swept down, swiveling around himself on the lightest of footsteps. Victor, mid-pirouette, spinning rapidly like a top. She felt his lips once again against hers, felt his arms around her, strong and safe—

The music had stopped. She sat on the ground, cello in her lap. She sucked in great heaving gasps of air. Hands touched her shoulder while faceless heads crouched and loomed nearby.

It took her far too long to realize *she* was the one screaming.

The whole world shook with her frantic sobs. The tag on her dress persisted in the same polite way she reminded herself of the facts: *Your boyfriend is dead and you are alone.* She recognized her father's voice close by, her sister, the other cellists, but grief swept their voices up and away, far out of reach.

Natalia clutched her cello as she'd clutched Victor's body in the street mere days ago, tears blurring out everything that was real, and screamed into the dark.

There was a soft knock at the door. Sitting in the corner of the shower with her legs hugged to her chest, Natalia stirred.

"Natalia?"

It was her mother. She didn't respond.

"Dinner's ready. Please come eat."

She sat staring through the foggy glass at her rumpled clothes on the floor for as long as she thought she could without worrying her mother. Then she dried herself off, dressed, and took slow steps downstairs.

Three weeks Victor had been dead, and with each minute her world came a little bit more undone.

She hadn't cried since her failed performance at his funeral. Sometimes she would feel the threat approach, but she'd squeeze her eyes shut tight against the flood, and lie on the floor of the shower for forty-five minutes instead. It was warm and unending, a kind of comfort she desperately longed for but couldn't find anywhere else.

The TV in the living room was muted on sweeping, magnificent views of a cruise ship on the travel channel. Natalia considered the pristine white ship. She imagined herself walking through the television and straight into the promised paradise onscreen. Escaping, in one fell swoop, from the misery that hovered around her, ready at any moment to snap closed and trap her within.

That wasn't how their magic worked. Performances and flashy tricks were the main draw, but those required a partner, while smaller, lesser tasks could be accomplished alone—like changing the color of a sweater, or encouraging a wilted flower to temporarily bloom. The magic wasn't a cure-all, despite her most fervent wishes.

"Natalia?"

Her family sat, waiting patiently, around the dinner table.

She sighed and took a seat. Her sister Juliana was still in her black leotard, straight from dance practice, and soft tendrils of the honey-blond hair they shared were slipping out of her bun. She offered Natalia a sympathetic smile and reached for the nearest bowl.

"We can eat now, right?"

Their father sighed. "Yes, Juliana."

Dinner was fine, at first. Natalia took the plate onto which her mother had spooned food for her and stared down at it: red beans and rice with sliced sausage, and an artful fan of sliced avocado in the center. It smelled great, but tasted like dryer lint to her dulled senses. She felt heavy, like something was dragging her down through the universe, knocking things apart, and sooner or later she'd hit rock bottom. But at least she wasn't sitting in the shower anymore.

"Natalia, I wanted to talk to you," her father began. She looked up at him blankly, thankful for an excuse not to eat. "I haven't heard any music from your room lately. Have you practiced?"

No, she hadn't practiced. How could she, when she was so accustomed to Victor's presence? To the way his graceful movements collided with her music and sent glittering sparks of magic into the air? What reason did she have to practice alone? All she could produce without a dancer was mere song, and her world had no room for song in its sucking gray depths.

Natalia cleared her throat. "No. I, um…no."

Her father nodded. "And why is that?"

Was he kidding?

"Victor is dead, Dad." Her words went around the table like a slap and tension descended to soothe the sting. "I have no use for the cello anymore. Not by myself. It's pointless."

He flinched as if she'd cursed at him. To call her gift pointless was next to blasphemy. In San Pacuí, musical or otherwise artistic gifts that lent themselves to magic were expected to be used as such. They all shared a duty to contribute. Without the steady flow of cash from tourists charmed by the lightly-magical atmosphere, the tiny seaside town wouldn't survive.

"So you mean to give it up entirely? Abandon years of instruction over some *boy*—"

"I'm not abandoning it. Just...setting it aside. Temporarily."

"They were together for two years," Juliana broke in quietly.

Her mother nodded in agreement. "Yes, David, please be reasonable. This was a serious relationship."

The pity in her mother's gaze was unbearable, a soft and rounded comfort in contrast to all her father's sharp edges. Neither of them seemed to fully grasp her grief. This wasn't a town where terrible things happened—until now. And she didn't know how to explain to them that Victor's death wasn't simply some minor setback she could easily overcome.

"I understand that," said her father, his tone softening even though his stare did not. "And we've given you plenty of time." Was there a time limit, she wondered, for grief? So far it had felt like one unending flood. "But Natalia, you need to contribute. We all depend on it. Magic is the only thing that keeps this town going."

As if she didn't know. As if they hadn't all lived with that pressure for years. Her parents had long since done their part, donating their magical gifts to the community efforts that kept the town running until those same magical gifts ran dry. Now, Natalia and her sister, and the rest of the younger generation, were responsible for taking up that mantle. Natalia heard the unsaid reprimand beneath her father's words: if she wasn't able to contribute during her most magically fertile years, what use did she even offer?

"I will. I know. I just need...time. I don't know. I don't—" The words sounded pathetic even to her. If time didn't help, what would? Maybe nothing. Her new and constant reality was a giant gaping hole in her life where Victor had always been. Maybe she would never make magic again. Maybe, because of her, the town would suffer.

Her attempts to explain herself only made her father wince. "I'm worried about you, that's all. You're drifting. Aimless. It's not good for you. Could you try the cello again? Or restart your dance lessons—just do *something*."

I am doing something. I took a forty-five-minute shower. I'm very clean.

Her mother gave her a gentle smile. "That might be a good idea. You used to enjoy dance, right? Why don't you give it another try?"

"Mom, I don't want—"

She fell silent, knowing it was useless. It was never about what she, or anyone, wanted. If she wasn't training or contributing, she might as well leave. But no matter how miserable her father's pointed persistence made her, she had nowhere else to go.

Having already humiliated her family once with her public breakdown, she needed to pull herself together to perform in the upcoming fall festival show. It was her one shot at redemption. The daughter of the town conductor could only be afforded but so much grace.

Natalia saw the truth of this in how quickly the conversation moved on. As she looked around the table, her father lifted a forkful of rice to his mouth. His jaw had relaxed as soon as he'd realized she wasn't going to put up a fight. He ate heartily now, unconcerned, chatting with her mother.

Juliana met her gaze. The corners of her mouth turned down as she mouthed to Natalia, *I'm sorry.*

Natalia reached under the table to squeeze her sister's hand. She picked at her food while the rest of them ate in silence.

⸺⟐⸺

"To the barre, please."

Forty perfect buns left the periphery of the room and gathered at the barre. Natalia chose a spot in the back corner of the room, near the end of one barre, its black paint cracked and peeling.

The instructor stood front and center. Her assistant, a girl with blue-brown skin and bright green braids halfway down her back, stood nearby, flexing her feet and rotating her ankles in her pointe shoes.

"We'll begin with *pliés*," said the instructor.

She walked them briefly through the combination, then strode over to the music system and selected a song. Piano notes streamed from the speakers, clear and sweet, ebbing and flowing in pace like rainfall.

Natalia tried desperately to remember the movements she'd just been shown. The other dancers moved effortlessly, almost as one. She was a beat behind as she sank into a deep squat, high on her toes, and struggled to get back up.

She didn't remember it being this difficult. In San Pacuí, those who showed signs of magic were funneled into training at a young age, gaining a broad knowledge of music, dance, and the visual arts. At twelve, she'd chosen the cello for her specialization, but she'd still been an excellent dancer. Ten years had passed since she'd stepped foot in a ballet class. A long time, but she'd imagined that her muscles would re-acclimate themselves more quickly, that she wouldn't feel such a tightness in movements that had once been so fluid.

"Left side," said the instructor.

Natalia watched those around her helplessly, and tried to mirror their timing.

She looked like a proper dancer, at least. Juliana had twisted her hair into a pristine bun. The tight knot pulled at the skin of her face whenever she moved. Her feet looked like everyone else's, ensconced in shiny pale pink with ribbons wrapping up her calf. In her leotard and tights, and the pale blue shrug she'd borrowed from her sister as well, she could see the weight that had disappeared along with Victor. Her collarbones were visible in a way they had never been before. She was just as skinny as the other dancers.

But she still stood out.

With every movement, her toes screamed in agony, and she imagined lakes of blood welling up inside her shoes, spilling up and over the tops and dripping down to the floor in an abstract painting. Everything felt off, and her grief dragged her down. It pressed in on her from the top of her head to her toes as if it wanted to squish her flat.

The instructor traveled the room, wandering up and down the aisles in between barres. She paused near the speakers as the song came to an end.

"Let's try a slow *tendu* now, shall we?"

The dancers turned to face the front once more. It was then that Natalia noticed the picture.

A large frame hung on the far left wall, depicting last year's performance of *Swan Lake*. Victor stood front left next to the swan queen. She remembered sitting in this same studio, humming the other melodies on top of her cello, watching as Victor rehearsed his role.

Panic crawled up her throat. Its fingers pressed against her insides, tickling the bottom of her mouth, grabbing at her tongue—

"Hey, you need some help?"

It was the assistant. She'd tied her green braids into a huge knot atop her head, and gave Natalia a helpful smile.

"Uh..." Natalia glanced around. She noticed the other dancers moving on to another exercise and realized she'd missed that cue entirely. Her head felt fuzzy.

"I'm Roxanna, by the way. Did you just join this class? I don't think I've seen you before."

She nodded. "I'm Natalia. Also, I haven't danced properly in ten years."

"Shit!" Roxanna glanced at her feet. "How are your toes doing?"

Natalia grimaced.

Roxanna shuddered. "I can't even imagine." She snuck a look at the others. "They've moved on to pirouettes now, but I want to make sure you got that *tendu* combination."

"Sure, thanks. That'd be great."

They worked together quietly for a few minutes before the instructor joined them.

"How are we doing over here?" she asked, looking warmly at Natalia. "I noticed we had a new face today. I am Madame Ksenia. Welcome."

"I'm struggling, but Roxanna's been a huge help so far."

"Of course. Watch after her Roxanna, *da*? I hate to watch a beautiful girl with so much potential struggle so terribly." She placed a hand on Natalia's shoulder. "You will get it, do not worry."

She was so unused to this kindness that tears welled in her eyes. "Thank you," she whispered.

About an hour later, they stepped out into the suffocating heat. The other dancers peeled away from the building in twos and threes, heading for the sidewalk.

"I think I want ice cream. Want to come?"

Natalia opened her mouth to say yes at the same time as she noticed her mother's car pulling into the lot. You could get anywhere in town on foot within fifteen minutes, but her parents were treating her like something that might spoil if exposed to the elements for too long. She felt faint stirrings of irritation each time it happened, but she understood. After Victor's death, she didn't trust herself either.

"I wish, but my mom's waiting," she said, gesturing lamely to the car.

Roxanna's face fell slightly. "Damn. Well, let me know if you need anything. I'm more than happy to meet with you outside of class if you want some extra help."

Natalia smiled her first real smile in what felt like the longest month of her life.

"Thank you. That would be amazing."

She said goodbye, and walked to her mother's car. Air conditioning wrapped her in its cool embrace as she stepped inside. Somewhere deep down, though, she still felt warm. As her mother signaled and pulled out onto the street, Natalia tore her eyes from Roxanna's back, her braids swishing from side to side as she walked through the crosswalk.

⸺◈⸺

Natalia pushed through the glass door of the studio and leaned against the doorframe, watching Roxanna move across the floor. The walls vibrated with the heart of an upbeat tune. She glanced down at her leotard, tights, and leg warmers and wondered if she had missed something.

"Uh…"

Roxanna paused, seeing her, and ran over.

"You're here!" she gushed. She slid the duffel bag off Natalia's shoulder, then pulled at her hands. "Come on! Let's get started."

Natalia allowed herself to be led to the center of the floor before feeling overwhelmed.

"I thought you were helping me with ballet?"

Roxanna grinned. "You did ballet for a while. It'll come back eventually. I figured we could have some fun today?"

She studied Roxanna's outfit: a large black tank top, multi-colored leggings that were loose around the thighs, and a plaid jacket tied around her waist.

"That depends. What does your definition of fun entail?"

"Wellll...I teach an intro hip-hop class on Saturday mornings, and last week I came up with choreography that I'm really proud of, and...it's really fun and I think you'll enjoy it!"

Natalia stared at her. The other girl's face was open and hopeful. Green eyeshadow shimmered on her dark skin above eyes that twinkled with excitement. The last thing she felt like doing was dancing to the song she'd just heard. Ballet, at least, was mostly comprised of soft, mellow piano tunes that fed on her sadness. Now she felt like she'd walked into some bizarre grief counseling camp, where everyone wore yellow and sang happy songs about how well-adjusted they were to the deaths of their loved ones. But she saw how thrilled Roxanna looked, and she couldn't bear to disappoint her. Even if she herself felt like nothing.

She let out a long sigh. "Fine. But only because you're begging like a puppy right now."

Giggling, Roxanna pulled a remote out of her pocket and restarted the song.

"Okay, watch."

It was exactly what she would have expected from an intro hip-hop class, which was why she'd stuck to ballet for so many years. Roxanna's choreography was high-energy. She bounced all over the place, hitting tiny beats in the music that were hardly noticeable and shaking parts of her body that Natalia preferred to keep in their traditional locations. It did look like fun, though.

She tried.

She watched Roxanna closely and mirrored her as best as she could. This was much faster than ballet, with much more opportunity for error, but somehow it didn't matter. If she forgot what came after the turn, she could just do what felt natural, and avoid standing motionless in a mental fuzz until she caught back up to the piano pattern, like she'd been doing in ballet.

Occasionally, she'd hear Victor's voice, or picture him grinning as she shook and shimmied and tripped over herself trying to keep up. She felt like an idiot, but with no one around to judge her other than Roxanna and the imaginary Victor in the corner of her eye, she had no excuse to stop.

And so they danced.

They met nearly every day for several hours at a time, usually after ballet. Natalia danced through the misery that woke her each morning with its crushing pressure on her chest. Slowly, she began to feel human again. Each day that she came home exhausted and covered in sweat, and got in and out of the shower within a reasonable amount of time, she felt a little bit better, though her cello sat unused in a corner of her room. Sometimes her father drove her to rehearsal in the mornings, and as they left the car and headed for their separate buildings, he'd give her a brief, approving nod or smile.

She spent an ever-increasing amount of time with Roxanna, whose presence made her calm and happy.

She wasn't sure who she was becoming, but it felt more right than anything she'd ever known.

"You've been using magic on your hair this whole time?"

Roxanna turned away from the mirror to peer over her shoulder. Her hair was out, full and curly and only green at the tips.

"Of course. Dye's expensive. And magic is less damaging."

Natalia grinned and came to sit near her on the bathroom counter.

"So if you don't do anything, it just fades back?"

"Pretty much." Roxanna removed the last of her braids and tossed the hair band into the sink on top of the others. She gave Natalia a meaningful look. "That's why I need you."

They both looked at Natalia's cello case where it rested near the door. It was covered in a light film of dust. She didn't remember it always being as heavy as it had been when she'd carried it over to Roxanna's place.

"I don't know if I can," Natalia said honestly. The more often she danced, the longer her cello sat, lonely, in its corner in her room. She hadn't played in ages and wasn't sure what it would sound like if she tried now.

"Can you try?" Roxanna turned to her, taking her hand. She felt her heart speed and slow, blood rushing to the spot where they touched. "If it's too much, I understand."

The magic was more efficient if the musician and the dancer had already practiced together for some time, and it would be easier if she helped, rather than forcing Roxanna to work with a stranger. As nervous as she was, she also hated the idea of Roxanna asking one of the musicians from her old class, hated the thought of their talents mixing together and sparking color into Roxanna's hair.

She sighed. "No, I'll do it."

Roxanna's resulting smile was reward enough.

Natalia went for her cello and set it up in the next room. Roxanna had pushed her bed and desk into the far corner to leave plenty of room for dance rehearsal. The last rays of sunset streamed in through the window, warm red-orange preparing to fade to cool violet. Roxanna came and stood in the vanishing light, tossing her hair with her hands.

Natalia lowered her head and stared at her cello.

"What should I play?"

"Whatever you like."

She brushed some of the dust off the smooth wood and flipped through her mental catalog of songs. Nothing particular came to mind, so she simply began to play. The melody poured out of her, swift and unexpected. Her fingers felt a little stiff, slightly clumsy, but the notes came from somewhere deep within, a well of inspiration she'd never known she had. For a while she watched Roxanna's shadow through half-lidded eyes, not daring to look. Then, slowly, she raised her gaze.

Roxanna danced, slowly and skillfully, as if the music absorbed into her skin. The song evolved with each turn of Natalia's thoughts, but Roxanna kept pace expertly, manipulating her weight into turns and leaps at a moment's notice. Muscles rippled under her skin. Her breath came in short gasps. Natalia was mesmerized. Her hands moved automatically on the cello, and her throat felt dry. She was unable to tear her eyes from Roxanna's long limbs arcing through the air.

Balls of light, a deep blue, began to form near the floor. They swirled and bounced along with the music, trailing Roxanna as she pressed herself into pirouettes. Warmth brushed against Natalia's own skin, making her gasp, and she glanced down to see bright yellow sparks flowing down her arms.

Her pulse grew frantic. The magic she'd long assumed dead along with Victor had started to work again. She wasn't broken. The possibility of it all became a lump in her throat, a tentative leaping in her chest.

Between them, blue and yellow met, mixing and intensifying, shifting to that signature shade of green. Natalia slowed the beat. The green sparks hovered momentarily in midair, then began to surround Roxanna. Her hair lifted and shone with energy. Excess magic sparked off the ends. Green spread from her hairline to the very tips. She turned one final time.

For a moment, after Roxanna had stopped dancing and Natalia's hands froze where they were, the world stood still, balancing on the edge of everything.

Roxanna turned and took the cello and bow from Natalia to gently set them on the floor. Then she reached for her hands and pulled her to her feet. Natalia heard her swallow, and suddenly they were kissing, warm and soft, Roxanna's hands cupping her face. The kiss raged through Natalia with a tender kind of fire. She pressed her hands into the small of Roxanna's back, damp with fresh sweat, and opened her mouth to Roxanna, in the way she hadn't known she wanted until that moment. The roar of her pulse drowned out every thought. Between them, the space felt electric, alive with leftover magic.

Natalia slid her hands up Roxanna's shirt, touching smooth skin, then slid the fabric off. She felt lips on her neck, hands holding her close, and her eyelids fluttered.

All of a sudden, Roxanna pulled away. Natalia opened her eyes, searching.

"You're crying," Roxanna said.

"Am I?" She hadn't realized. "I—I'm sorry. I don't know if I can—"

"Is it because of—"

Natalia cut her off before she could say his name.

"I'm sorry—I'm so sorry—I really like you but—"

"Too soon?"

She nodded.

Roxanna gave her a small smile, placing a hand on her cheek.

"It's okay. Don't worry about it." Her thumb brushed over Natalia's lips, wiping away tears.

"I'm so sorry."

"Don't apologize."

They stayed like that for a long moment, holding each other close. Natalia fought the urge to kiss her once more. Every inch of her screamed for it, but she was worried she'd cry again. Instead, she stepped away and picked up her cello.

"Dance for me?" she asked.

Roxanna raised an eyebrow, looking down at her bare chest. "Like this?"

Natalia nodded and resumed her seat near the cello. "Just like that," she said, and began to slide her bow across the strings.

Natalia lay motionless in bed, forcing her eyelids closed and allowing the darkness to swallow her whole. If she remained perfectly still, perhaps her overactive brain would shut itself off, and she'd be able to sleep, but that hadn't happened yet.

Victor, dead, was intruding more persistently than he ever had while alive. Usually, his presence was welcome. It calmed her to wake up imagining him at her side, hogging the shower in his tiny apartment, spoon-feeding her fried potatoes hot off the stove. If she couldn't have him in the real world, then having him in her mind was often enough.

Now, though, she wasn't sure she wanted him. She wanted to focus during ballet class, rather than diligently ignoring his portrait hanging in the room and later coming undone when she could no longer resist the urge to look. She wanted to spend hours out of the day with Roxanna, dancing, kissing, talking, laughing—without the thought of Victor taking away from that. She still loved him, of course, and she probably always would.

But she wanted her life back.

Natalia sighed and rolled over to look at her clock. 2:42 AM. She sat up, groaning. The faint outline of her cello stared back at her from the corner. Frustrated, she got up to switch on her desk lamp and then stared accusingly at her cello, hands on her hips. She hadn't felt an urge to play just for herself since before losing Victor. Everything since then—playing at the funeral, helping with Roxanna's hair—she'd had to cajole herself into, bit by bit.

Tonight, the instrument called out to her. Her fingers itched for the bow and the taut pressure of the strings. Cursing under her breath, she opened the case and pulled a chair over.

She felt ridiculous, sitting braless with proper posture in loose shorts and a sleeping t-shirt with a puppy on the front. But she lowered the bow to the strings all the same.

It started off shaky. Without the lingering emotion of Victor's funeral or Roxanna dancing right in front of her, she had little motivation, and her songs felt empty. The cello sounded healthy and sweet, but she felt nothing from within, no connection to the sounds she produced.

She stopped. Music fell off into the silence of the night.

Natalia took a deep, steadying breath. She tried again.

This time, she went back to the day of Victor's death. They had been walking the streets in the next town over when they'd stumbled upon a parade. Hundreds of people spilled from the sidewalks into the roads, singing and dancing and blocking out the sky with figures mounted on stilts. The world came alive with color and sound, a stark contrast to the peaceful day they'd been hoping for. Those in the parade sang in a dialect neither of them were familiar with, and the crowd grew quickly. One moment, Victor's hand was squeezed tightly around hers, pulling her, hopefully, towards somewhere less populated. Then he was gone, lost in the sea of the crowd. She stood frozen, a rock in a rushing river, searching for him, yelling his name.

Minutes passed. She heard the brakes of a car screech to a stop, and an abrupt cease to the parade's music. Screams began, first one and then many, many more, like dominoes falling rapidly toward an end she couldn't foresee. She pushed through people in the direction of the noise. Somehow, by the sinking feeling in her stomach, she already knew, but when she saw how the crowd had gathered around the fallen body, her world shattered into fragments.

A distraught man climbed from his car and made excuses. Natalia stared right past him, then dropped, knees smashing to the asphalt as she fell next to Victor. Dark red seeped from a gash in his head and from beneath his stomach. He reached for her weakly. Blood bubbled and spilled from his lips. She gathered him into her arms. The parade slowed around her until the pressure of so many curious eyes became almost too much, but she stayed where she was until the police arrived and gently pried her, kicking and screaming, from Victor's body.

Now, tears streamed down her face, dripping into her mouth as she sobbed. No longer conscious of the melody she made, she let it sweep her along, hands moving automatically. She felt jagged, raw. Like something sharp that needed to be repaired or discarded.

Suddenly, she felt a warm tingle near her sternum, and looked down to see red light rising from her chest. The magic swirled up from her heart and over her fingers on the cello, glittering around the strings. Shock almost stilled her fingers, but she pressed on, intrigued.

She wasn't supposed to be able to do this alone. Solitary magic was small and tepid, nothing like this. Magic was meant to be used in pairs, or large groups—an entire stage of dancers or an orchestra. It was more vibrant that way, more thrilling for the tourists.

Somehow, in her grief, she'd found a garbled shortcut to the flashy kind of power no one believed possible.

When her tears for Victor ran dry, and the magic ebbed, dipping down toward the floor, she thought of her frustration from earlier, how she'd been so eager for Roxanna but hadn't been able to disconnect from her residual longing and sadness for Victor. He was dead, and she had accepted that. She needed to move on and was annoyed with herself that she couldn't.

The magic surged upward, swirling from red into blue and orange and purple. She felt its glittering energy in her entire body, the hair on her arms and neck standing on end. It was a terrifying, beautiful feeling, and it exhausted her in its intensity.

At last, she lay her cello and bow on the floor. Clammy, chilled with cold sweat, the reality of the newfound ability stuttered around her center.

It had been so long since she had felt this powerful or capable.

She glanced at the sheet music inside her cello case that her father had distributed weeks ago in preparation for the fall festival, when she had all but given up.

Natalia reached for the papers and picked up her cello once more.

⸺⸺◈⸺⸺

Backstage at the auditorium, Natalia studied herself in the mirror. She wore a cream-colored, blue flower-print dress, secured around the middle with a thick black sash and bow. She'd curled her hair and pulled it into a tight ponytail, one tendril hanging down on the side.

Today, she would be strong.

She left the mirror and strode through the hallways in search of her father, the heels borrowed from Roxanna clacking with every step. The noise grounded her and helped her legs feel solid when everything else was mush.

She finally located him near the men's dressing room, talking to the children's conductor. Upon seeing her, he did a double take.

"Natalia. You look wonderful," he said, smiling.

"I'm playing first chair cello tonight."

His smile faltered. "I'm not sure—"

"I can do it, Dad. I've been practicing. I know you've heard me. I'm not going to mess it up again."

He studied her. She wondered if he was replaying her failed performance from months ago in the same way she had over the past few nights. She couldn't blame his uncertainty. But this was something she had to do.

"Are you sure? I'm worried you feel pressured to return to your spot. You can take your time, as long as you continue practicing."

Her legs trembled. If he said no, she wasn't sure she had the strength to be defiant.

A warm hand slipped into hers and squeezed. She looked over to see Roxanna.

"She can do it. Give her a chance. Please."

Her father's gaze traveled from Roxanna to Natalia to their clasped hands in between. She saw the exact moment he caught on. His eyes widened. For a moment, she was sure this was the end. She waited for his verdict to come down and crush into dust not just one, but several of the things that would make her happy.

He smiled at her.

"All right. I'll let the others know." Turning to Roxanna, he said, "It's nice to finally meet the person who returned the old Natalia to me."

With that, he left. Natalia almost fell over with the weight of her relief. Roxanna was positively beaming. She tugged Natalia closer for a brief kiss, soft and sweet. The lights dimmed to let them know it was close to showtime.

Suddenly, everything seemed terrifyingly real.

"You can do this," Roxanna said. "I'll be in the wings. Right over there." She pointed.

Natalia nodded. The orchestra began to fill the hallway, heading for the stage. With the rest of the cellists behind her, supportive voices at her back, she followed the path to the stage.

The hallways opened up into the open-air auditorium she'd disgraced mere months ago. It looked as if every seat was full, yet people were still filing in, taking places in the rows and standing near the back. The fall festival firework show was always their biggest crowd.

She took her spot on the stage with the other cellists. They were set to open the performance—just music, no dancers yet. The fireworks would begin after their song.

Natalia settled into her seat, smoothing out the folds of her dress. She adjusted the music on her stand and raised her bow to the ready position. Her father stepped up before the orchestra. Their eyes met, and he gave her a nod.

She could do this.

He signaled the beginning. Natalia and the other cellos jumped into an upbeat song. The audience tittered in recognition. It was a pop song from the radio, a departure from their usual classical pieces, but it had been Roxanna's suggestion. Over long hours of practice, the song had become sacred to her, and she wanted to share it with the world.

She had also been practicing something on her own: a bit of a surprise for the others. After tonight, her secret would be no more. As far as she knew, no one in the community had ever managed it before, but all she'd had to do was hold her cello tight and play from her heart, play for Victor, and Roxanna, and all the others that she loved. She hoped she could pull it off again.

Halfway through the song, she closed her eyes. She looked within, and drew on the strength she now knew herself to have. The broken person she had been after Victor's death was gone. Song and dance had helped to put her back together. Warmth suffused her arm, and without even looking, she knew the sparkling magic was there.

Twin ripples of shock went through both the orchestra surrounding her and the dancers, including Roxanna, who waited backstage. She opened her eyes to dumbfounded faces. Hands moved automatically on instruments, though all eyes were on her. The audience, assuming her glow resulted from some kind of special effect, began to cheer.

Others knew the truth. And that truth sang out loud and clear. Lights rose up from her skin, swirling into vibrant greens and blues and purples. Then, with a trailing hiss and a whistle, Natalia's magic exploded into the sky.

Her magic, reclaimed, sparkled with such intensity it became fireworks. Her own personal pyrotechnics. With the jagged edges of Victor's death serving as kindling, she was left one step closer to healing.

Natalia smiled—for real, this time—and let the thrum of her cello sweep her away.

The Loneliness of Former Constellations

P.H. Low

This story appeared previously in Strange Horizons

When the doorbell first rings, I do not rise from my chair.

It is one of those days when the hurt bends me double. My nerves pulse sharp behind my eyelids; my fingers, clenched around the worn wooden armrests, are full of thorns. But outside the open window, the maples blaze a vermilion song—and so, at the bell's second chime, I hobble down the hall, raise myself to the peephole.

I have only ever seen her in two dimensions: bright pixels on a small glass tablet I would have laughed at, once, for its primitiveness. Here, it is all I have.

In person, her hair is red as the leaves. And she is so, so young.

"Come in," I say, cracking open the door. She hefts a huge trunk—the kind with leather straps and no wheels, wide as she is tall—and cocks her head.

"You're Hedi?"

"Yes."

"Are you really a house witch?"

Despite the ache unfurling in my chest, I smile. That she might give me such a name, trapped as I am in this flesh I did not choose.

"You could say so." I flex my fingers, and her mouth crooks as the chandelier above my head flares bright, every pale candle. Heat waxes across my shoulder blades, drips down. I am too tired to wince. But it's worth the effort.

"Impressive," she says, and thrusts her hand toward mine with a modicum more respect. "I'm Alanna."

"Well met," I say, shaking. Her grip is flawless—long-fingered and strong.

—◆—

This is the house: three floors of shining mahogany, lintels of flowered marble, rafters and windows arched as the sky. Lightbulbs gutter in sconces, installed at the dawn of mass production; dried roses hang like dark exhales above the main fireplace.

All mine, for years. But too large, of late, for a single person and her sleepless turning.

And when I tripped down the stairs one night, lay for hours gasping and panting on the floor as the nanites in my bones knit me back together, I decided it would be good to have another person nearby. Another body. Just in case.

"How long have you lived here?" Alanna strides ahead of me through the main hall, a dark blur of leather jacket, black jeans, combat boots. She has the ramrod posture of someone the world cannot tamp down—thirty years old, maybe, or thirty-five.

"Longer than you've been alive," I say.

Her eyes flick up: the dark blue of an old friend's, long gone. "You don't look a day over twenty."

When I attempt a shrug, my shoulders sing lightning, and my eyes water. I point to my chair, still out of reach. "If you would be so kind—"

"Oh. Here." A soft thud on the wooden floor, a guiding hand, and my legs fold into the cushions.

"Thank you." I tip my head back into the draft-cooled headrest, breathe. "Sorry. I'm—it's not the best of days."

"Ah."

"I should have told you—"

"No," she says, knife-sharp. "You didn't have to."

"I take care of everything, regardless." I curl my fingers again. A slow convulsion beneath my sternum, and the tea kettle whistles. I'd heated it up earlier in anticipation, but still. "Would you like some tea?"

"That would be lovely, but—" Her voice catches. "Are you sure you don't need—?"

"Please, sit." When I clench my fist, the whistling stops. Two china cups clink down on the dining table, Italian blue. "Breakfast or Earl Grey?"

"Earl Grey," she says quickly, and I laugh, heaving back to my feet. She holds out a hand to urge me back down, but the house parts for me in its subtle way, slants its generous floors to help me along.

"Good. I was out of Breakfast anyway."

⸻ ❖ ⸻

The next morning, I take my usual walk through the garden. A cold wind blows through, wild geese skimming fast and low across the sky, and it's going to be a good day. I can feel it in my spine, in the mud squelching between my bare toes. It rained overnight, and the grass is beaded with dew, the maples shaking off droplets with every gusted breeze. It lulled me as I lay in bed, in the early blue hours, and for once I did more than close my eyes.

When I turn on the path, a black sedan has rolled up on the driveway. The flame of Alanna's hair bobs across the asphalt, the straight shadow of her trunk in hand, and the door clicks shut, smooth as patent leather.

I had expected a horse, when she told me about her day job. Had expected clanking gauntlets, long walks on supple leather boots, merry bands of travelers. The essence of this country's dreams, in particular, have been slow to change.

But I suppose a car does make things easier.

I blink, and wind moans through the trees. Blink and the driveway is empty again, the road still as yesterday.

⸻ ❖ ⸻

I spend the afternoon in my chair, stringing together poems like strands of pearls. Supper's at four, on plates I wash by hand when I am done: honey on soft white bread, cheese cubes petaled with almond slices. Evening by the fire, a mug of chamomile tea warm in my palms.

This is my exile: it may be interminable, but I do not see why it must be spent in agony.

At night, the house groans, slow, like a tree broken by wind. I remember crystal spires and eyes like seas, and hold my breath until my vision blurs.

Two days later, I find myself gripping the banister of the third floor, my forehead slick with sweat.

I have not been up here since my final preparation for Alanna's move-in. Dust has gathered on the banister, the light slanting through the high windows brittle and blue with coming winter. I had forgotten how bright it was. How it feels to peer down to the living room and imagine that, if I jumped, I could fly again.

But I'm here to clean—have been paid to keep cleaning, an extra (albeit meaningless) two hundred dollars added to Alanna's deposit in the app—so I unclench my fingers and roll up my sleeves.

Alanna's quarters are neater than one might expect, from one so young. Her leather jacket is draped over a chair, traded out for the black coat that billowed as she crossed the driveway; a bag of robes and body armor gapes at the foot of the bed. On the bookshelf, swords are balanced elegant as the bows of violins, a square of crimson cloth draped over the longest of them in mid-polish.

A knot forms in my rib cage. What it must be to vanquish so easily, with a blade of steel and the weapon that is your body. What a rush, to plunge toward death with the whole of your being, free of the fear of one who has been broken.

When I open my palm, a bellflower rests in its center: a cracked algorithm, cells programmed to reach toward light as well as warmth. Its pollen scatters gold across my skin.

I close my fingers around it and take up the cleaning cloth with my other hand.

———⬦———

That evening, Alanna bursts through the front door in a whirl of groceries and fallen leaves.

"Hello," she says, beaming, and I smile back, though my spine is a riot of pain. Marigolds have grown across my back to pad it, carnations strained through my fingertips, and their stems twine me to my chair.

"Hello," I echo, and her paper bag of bread and vegetables lands, hard, on the floor.

"Are you okay?"

"Yes." I have always been told I have an exhibitionist streak. But it has been a long time since anyone has asked after my flowers.

I am a sapling starved of light. I am a house worn thin by the feet of ghosts.

I *cannot* expect her to fix me.

Alanna shrugs off her coat and steps closer, eyes wide. "May I—?"

My throat lumps: an owl pellet of abandon, hideously dead. "Yes."

Her fingers trace leaf, petal, calyx, gentle as spring sun. I close my eyes.

"Thank you," I say, soft, even though she was the one who asked. I swallow. "Also, I cleaned."

"Thanks," she says, her right cheek dimpling, and then she draws away.

She slots broccoli into the refrigerator, the line of her back straight and unyielding. Hard to believe she is the young one, and I am what I am.

I sip my tea. The heat scorches me numb.

"How was your week?" I try.

"I killed a wyvern that was terrorizing a village." Alanna reaches up—overly intent, her head cocked at too steep an angle—to place a jar of honey on the high shelf. "The mayor gave a speech in my honor, after."

"Ah," I say. "Good."

The tips of her ears flush pink.

She begins to return, after that, with her face streaked in blood, robes acrid with ashes. I learn I am not the only exhibitionist in this house; nestled in my chair, swathed in rosehip warmth and curling leaves, I ask how, and why.

It's the griffins, she tells me as she oils her swords—they maul fisheries, ravage the parks. Basilisks hiss down subway tunnels; malicious spirits manifest under full eclipse. Humans overween, overgrow, but there are still children to protect, and cities.

There is still a war to fight, and she wields one of the few blades left to fight it.

I do not ask, as she plunges into the next battle and the next, why she does not instead find out how to make more blades. No: she speaks of her next adventure, her next conquest, and I drink in her words like honey.

On a day that dawns bitter and cold as the sea, she returns with a clean sword.

"I've found the Ancient One," she tells me, and I recognize the fever in her eyes: the heady anticipation of knowing your time has come, that even the barest tilt of your face—cheekbone, forehead, jaw—bears the weight of watching history. I pressed my lips to such a forehead, once. "I'll be gone for awhile."

"Be careful," I say, despite myself, and her right cheek dimples.

"Always."

⟡

That night, clasped between her door and the lens of her cell phone camera, she confides to someone—someones?—in a voice thick with hope and fear.

"I can't believe this is really happening," she says, and I am not one to eavesdrop, but the wind has hushed, and the house pricks at the faintest sound like a jealous lover. "I started this search ten years ago. Now—"

I steeple my fingers and rock in my chair before the hearth. My carnations have shriveled to seed, marigolds melted back into skin. Only the dried roses above the mantel see my eyes blur, my wrist crooked to wipe them dry.

I am waiting—but not for her.

The absence of voices echoes beneath my skin.

I have waited for so long.

Hours later, when the fire has dimmed to sullen embers, her door cracks open. She pads down the stairs in a grey oversized t-shirt and sock feet. Pauses on the fourth step, seeing me.

"Still up?" she asks, sleep-soft.

I blink the heat from my eyes. Words furl in the pit of my throat, unravel on my tongue. I want to tell her about space—its incomprehensible vastness, planets devoured in a blink, data-scattered leaps between ships of fractal glass. I want to tell her about the speed of thought, and how, folded into math, whole minds might be tucked bright and sharp in the socket of a right eye.

I want to tell her about the Emperor, and the day I hurled him from his throne.

Instead I say, "I do not sleep."

"Ah."

She stays for a long, silent minute. Only when it becomes clear I have nothing more to add does she tiptoe back up the steps, the bones of her ankles flexed delicate and strong above her socks.

———◈———

She is gone again before sunrise.

The house should not feel strange without her. She is barely in it—a carton of unsweetened soy milk in the fridge, an extra pair of boots on the shoe rack, a faint aura of lavender. Yet in her absence, time uncurls slow as oak leaves in a dry season; days clench like buds in frost.

I walk into town to buy tea. I whisper to the climbing roses to grow their thorns sharp and wicked as the teeth that would consume them.

I do not think.

This body—this hungry, feeble flesh—was built to forget. Shivering on the garden path, I close my eyes, and for a moment I am only wind, rustling through grass; the pip of a cardinal, brave and dying. There is no Council, frowning down from glass balconies. No weapons thrumming eager and sure beneath my skin.

No operating table, scored with squares like a giant game of Go.

The war is over, they said, scalpels glinting like teeth. *You are a liability, now.*

We will remake you.

And I? I said yes, for the war I had won them, for a coalition I sifted together from their ashes.

That's what tickles them, still: that I, victorious, could have been such a fool.

When I open my eyes, I am empty as the waiting driveway, as a room on the third floor.

I said this body was built to forget.

I meant, rather, that the Council coded oblivion into this new flesh of mine, and in my war to remember, I deny myself reprieve.

Once, cities fell at a snap of my fingers. Once, starships shattered at a breath. But the Council chained me to flesh and algorithms half-stitched and porous as sponges, laid me out on a grassy hill as the burnt slag of my old arsenal leaked out of my ears.

The more I reach for it now, for even its paltry remainder, the more quickly I am torn apart.

On the tenth day, the front door slams, and in the thunder of footsteps up the stairs, I catch a stifled sob.

"Alanna?"

The light outside has faded, gold-limned maples shaded to indistinct indigo. I have been dozing by the window; when I uncrook my neck, something twangs, discordant.

It is late. She does not need my rescue.

My hip pops back into place, and the pain shears my vision white. "Here we go," I tell the house, and start up the stairs.

Stairs are tricksters in the dark. Two curving flights and I am ready to pray on stiff knees, I am ready to weep at what this will cost me. Still, I climb. Grip the banister, haul, stub a toe. I contemplate illumination, but am too tired to light the chandelier, too far up to reach back for the switch. I focus on Alanna's sobs. On my own pale, strange-shaped feet, so narrow and lacking in joints. Left, right. Grunt, push.

I am not being paid for this. Did not tap the agree box to these terms and conditions. But I cannot simply sit back and sip tea.

I want to help. I want too much.

I am not the one who needs healing.

"Alanna." My knuckles rap the door, hollow and clear. My nightshirt is plastered to my back with sweat. "Do you require immediate medical attention?"

A garbled mutter that I generously construe as *go away*.

"May I come in?"

"No."

I push open the door anyway. A bloom of open bandage, in the fading light: her arm has been slashed open from elbow to wrist, and the wound froths a toxic blue.

"Why didn't you call—" I start, but one look at her face and I know. It is the way I felt when I was dinged by a powder bullet on Olmmagar, or when a Derian viper nearly cored me with fangs long as knives. Those were primitive worlds, lesser wounds. They didn't deserve my pain.

I lower myself onto the bed, arms shaking, and pat the covers beside me. "You've sustained a great deal of nerve damage by waiting. Come here."

She scuttles away, cradling her arm. "Don't touch me."

"You'll die otherwise."

"You don't understand," she snarls, and her teeth are slicked red, her skin a pallid grey. "It knows my scent now, the sound of my footsteps. If I go back, it'll hear me coming from a thousand miles away."

"So?"

"I failed, all right?" One side of her face spasms, and she clutches her mauled forearm tighter. "I did what I came to do, and I fucked up, and now it's over." She lifts her chin, and were she not so young and covered in blood, she could have been a Council member, a paragon of ruling grace.

Could have been a weapon, aeons ago, in proud slow footsteps toward an operating table.

"You can still live," I say.

She laughs, scornful. "The way you do?"

The silence congeals.

There is a rage buried so deeply in some soldiers' souls that it ashes them from the inside—a rage so long in building that, once it erupts, it lights whole worlds on fire. That rage does not well in me now. When I sit back on the mattress, I am cold walls listening, I am the beating hollow of a heart, I am a cardinal hunched beneath skimming clouds, dark-eyed and watchful. I reach for fury and find it gone, its last curl of steam dissolved skyward with the first trains a century past.

There is no space left in this body to mourn.

"I'm sorry," Alanna mutters.

I lean forward, clench against the slow fire that cascades down my back. "Listen to me."

Her blood drips onto the floorboards.

"I was a weapon of my people," I say. The words are strange in my mouth—rendered in this thin high voice, fragile as lace. "I led nations in battle against the greatest Emperor of our age. I have swallowed suns and crushed moons to powder, ransomed worlds and resurrected kings. When the Army of Twelve rose up, I vivisected each of their commanders, in their own locked quarters, over twelve consecutive nights. And when we won the war, do you know what I did?"

Alanna blinks, blank.

"I became this." I spread my arms, encompassing soft thin biceps, penetrable rib cage. Corrupted code pulses behind my eyelids, and my hands fall back into my lap, limp. "I let them lay me down—for the sake of the new Coalition, for a treaty that promised disarmament—and by the time I realized what they were doing, they had broken off every piece of myself I had considered worth living for.

"I know what it is to lose," I say, and my voice is an empty shell aching for the sea. "Do not dare think, even for a moment, that you are the only one."

She looks away, then. Scans the room as if she will need to draw its every edge from memory. Her fingernails have withered to black.

"Alanna," I say, sharper, and she flinches as if struck. "It is your decision. But I do not think you should make it while half your blood is outside your body. And I would prefer not to bury my first tenant with the roses, as much as they would love to have you."

She makes a strangled sound, half moan. A tear rolls down her cheek.

I peel myself off the bed, clench bedpost and then bookshelf as my knees and ankles fold to the floor. Blood seeps into my pants, still warm.

"It's hard," I say. Leaves fill my mouth, and thorns, but for once I do not choke. "It's so hard. I know."

She crumples into me all at once—the fever and the shiver of her, a cry like the end of the world. Gripping her wrist, I tease out the poison. Leaked equations hone in on the bright twist of corrupted cells; queries smaller than an eyeblink tear in and root out. My lungs burn. The hilt of her sword digs into my hip. I am a sky stripped of atmosphere, an imploding star, obliteration. In all my years in this body, I have never hurt like this.

Hours or lifetimes later, her cries ease. Her head slides from my shoulder into my lap, and her eyes flutter closed, sweat-sheened.

She is, by the slow pulse at her throat, asleep.

I lift my head. The room reeks of salt and crimson, and even the waning dusklight bashes mallets across my temples. My legs are boneless sacks of flesh, my spine a nonentity.

Outside, crickets sing, surviving.

I lean away from Alanna's half-open mouth and vomit into a pool of her blood.

I twitch awake from a nightmare, my tongue a corpse, and smell roses.

I cleaned up before I passed out. I remember this, at least: the blood and toxins leached away by forgiving walls. The window cracked open without force, without bidding, to let in a breeze.

The rosebud curve of her upper lip.

I look up.

Alanna lies on the bed, her right arm crooked against her rib cage like a baby bird. The wound has sealed: a built-in end process, embedded in acid code. Scars will remain, as they do in all flesh.

As for her other wounds—

I do not think she will forget. I do not know if she will turn from here into silent forests or the clash of louder swords. If she will choose, tomorrow, to walk onward or away.

The war is over, they said.

The war does not end.

I untangle my arms from my legs—a geologic slowness, every muscle a bruise—and think: *she is still so young.*

⎯⎯◈⎯⎯

The next morning, I find a note on the counter, an ivory square of parchment printed in ink.

Thank you.

And, on the underside, in ballpoint scrawl: *Tea tomorrow at four?*

I write beneath it in fountain pen. The house has grown full of them over the years, alongside the roses: pens tucked into drawers and notebooks, curved and shining.

Ink blooms from this one's nib, dark and cold as a freshwater spring.

Yes.

⎯⎯◈⎯⎯

After tea, we go on a walk. It will be a short one—I realize this the moment my foot clenches against the grass, resisting—but we stagger anyway into the fading sun, lean on each other's shoulders as evening kisses the roses black.

In the living room, she shows me her swords, her stances. Her hands are warm on my elbows, and I sway, overcome.

"Don't tell me they never use sabers in space," she says, and I shake my head, quench a strangeness in my knees that is not pain.

"Our weapons were smaller," I say, unsteady. Her left palm still rests on my shoulder, a small flame. "Subatomic. Linguistic. Or vast as suns."

"Tell me."

I hand her the blade—she takes it, silently, as I curl back into my chair—and tell her about my old crew: our joining together out of abandoned cargo stations and adamantine cryoholds. The fiery bloom of starship battles in six dimensions, pale armies imploding with our names on their lips. The vine-thick pulse of our interwoven minds as we marched on the Emperor's palace.

As I speak, memory patters like stones down my spine. Voxel teeth scrape the underside of my skin. I think of true names, though I do not speak them aloud; recall fists raised in salute to a resistance that promised us peace, a people we thought would love us for our bravery.

We were so, so young.

Alanna stuffs her hand in her pocket, the one that cannot grip the hilts of her old blades for too long. The toxin was ancient and cunning, and I could not rebuild the nerves it had already burned away. "What happened to them after the war?"

"There was no after, for them," I say, and though the void yawns inside me, I do not weep. This is a fact; it has been, for an age. In the end, it hurts more to rise again from my chair—to clutch its arm, wobbling. That I should stand in their honor, now, at the end of the world. That they might see, or care. "They died in the Emperor's throne room. He peeled them open and ate them organ by organ, as I watched."

She doesn't blink. "And *then* you killed him? By yourself?"

"They gave me something of themselves, in death." I look to the fire. Strange, that their screams should be memorialized in this vibration of air against thin epiglottis, that the thunder of our joined minds be drowned out by a crackle of flame against hearth. "Only then, when we were truly one, could we wrest him from the throne."

"I see." Alanna's mouth hardens. Limned by fire, she is a knight cast in gold, she is a song made flesh, and I want to hold her, to fall into her—to be harbor and harbored, shelter and sheltered.

There should be no consolation for one such as me. I cannot be her responsibility, or she the balm to this unrelenting need.

But this—this, her hand coming to the nape of my neck, the other trembling at my wrist—and my breath hitches anyway.

"You should sit." Her eyes are blown wide and dark. "Your legs are shaking."

I look down at my knees and do not see them. "Are they?"

"Yes," she says, mock-stern, and lowers me gently back into the cushions. "Perhaps it's time to turn in for the night."

Neither of us moves. Wind groans through the rafters.

The abyss in my bones gapes a million light-years wide.

"No," I say at last. "I haven't finished."

The windowsill creaks as she settles onto it. "Well, go on, then."

I breathe in through my nose, exhale to the hummingbird of my heart. There is a part of me that does not want to remember anymore. That no longer wants to hurt. That looks down at the narrow softness of this body and sees only the claim it will make on me in the end.

Once upon a time, I carried death under my skin. Now it is a dream half-faded on waking.

"When it was over, we looked around at the carnage," I say, quietly. "We saw the Coalition we were going to build. But when the many worlds had come to an agreement, when the Council changed us, I didn't truly believe they would take everything. I didn't believe they would take *them*." My voice breaks, a reed against a wall, and then the void blooms across my skin and I was not made to cry, not designed to, but I do it anyway, five hundred years of silence broken against the stone in my throat, against my hand stretched into this planet's just-blooming internet and returned less empty, against the inconsolable passing of days and winters and never knowing whether this semblance of life, this bridge to nowhere, will one day be memory.

"Hush." I barely see her move—only a cool gust of aftermath, and then her forehead is pressed to mine, her eyes like black glass. I breathe, and breathe again. There is not enough air. "Shhh," she says. "Shhh. Let it out."

Heat streaks down my cheek. "I don't know how to do this."

A shadow of a laugh. "You say it like I do." And then she holds me, her right hand twitching against my back, and doesn't let go.

I think about how the *we* who hurled the Emperor into deep space would be ashamed. I think of the Councilors smug in their high glass chambers, secure in a power we willingly handed over. But tucked against this falling night, as ghosts swim the oceans between my ribs, I let myself fall, let this soft, precarious body run its inscrutable course, and when I raise my head again, Alanna's eyes are bright as stars.

Winter is hard.

Shut in the house, snow thick across our driveway, Alanna paces, hurls her swords against the wall with her scarred hand: *too slow.* I knead my stiff back, feet cold against the cold floor, and haul myself up and down the stairs.

We cannot do this, I think whenever she breaks, or I do. *Neither of us is enough.*

Yet she stays. Yet I do not disintegrate from the sheer enormity of time and unknowing. We fall to our knees and breathe together, slow, shivering, and then we help each other up and make tea.

"You see that?"

Deep winter: the sky burned white, snowdrifts fluffed extravagant around tarp-wrapped maples. We have cut the roses and hung them throughout the house, and the garden is luminous with the scent of severed stems, arched and clean as coming spring.

"What?" I ask, leaning against her shoulder.

Alanna pulls a black hat tighter over her ears. A young man bought it for her, the last time we went into town—because he thought her pretty, or because he pitied my presence at her side, I couldn't tell. Either way, she accepted it, and we went on our way. "Over the hills, there."

She points, and time stops, and the sky is a glass a breath away from tipping.

It's a ship. A Phrian runner, the gouge in its hull familiar as my own reflection, shields ashen with the fire of reentry. By the time it has circled twice, thrice, and settled on the nearest hill, I am stumbling through the snow.

"Hedi," Alanna says. "You know them?"

"I—" The stone in my throat swells, hardens. "I don't know."

"Shall we find out?"

When I nod, she takes my hand and we fly down the slope, and it barely hurts at all.

At the top of the next hill, the door to the ship slides open, and a laugh falls out of me like a thunderclap.

Striding down the walkway is a stranger: the cut of her eyes and mouth a distorted shadow of faces I once fought beside, the line of her shoulders an echo of my heart's own shape. Her knuckles are not yet knotted with scars, and her irises swirl silver-green instead of blue. But when she calls me by my true name—when she pulls me into an embrace, her jacket smelling of fire and scorched steel—I have to fight the sob that cracks out of my throat.

"You don't know how long we've been looking for you," she says, pulling back to examine me, though the second lenses over her eyes have already taken their impressions—cross-section, chemical composition, circuitry or lack thereof. I search them anyway, for pity, for the old grief, and find nothing. Not yet. "A couple anti-Council hackers grew a bunch of us—" she motions at herself— "from the remains in the Emperor's throne room, and sent us out across the galaxy."

"They—they *sent*—" The wind buffets my ears. I cannot speak. A bubble is rising in my chest, softer than pain, but as deep.

That it should be this simple. That all my waiting should have come to this.

"So you're not—"

"Unfortunately, no," the stranger says, and I do not know whether to shout or cry or fall, as I have been far too prone to, lately, back into the forgiving snow. "They scavenged what they could, but we don't have the Myriads' memories. Just the seeds of their bodies." She flexes one arm and I choke on a laugh, startled at the familiarity of the gesture. "We can refuel at Yaito, grab drinks at the Starboard. There are many who would like to see you in person."

Beside me, Alanna asks, "Would you have room for one more?"

I turn.

This winter has molded her into something different—not simply softer, or sharper, but worn, the way a stone is tumbled against the sea floor until its face is thumb-smooth. Now, though, there is an old hunger in her gaze. Tempered by time, yes, but not gone.

"You spoke of ships that sail in six dimensions," she reminds me. "Secrets to shatter cities."

"I did," I say, wary.

"Can anyone wield them?"

"You could, theoretically," I say, even as heat carves a crescent down my rib cage. A new fault line is cracking open inside me. I want to take her hand again. I want to drag her back down the hill. I want to be sipping tea with her in the sitting room as rain taps at the windows, safe from worlds that demand more than we can ever give. "Given some upgrades. And proper training."

The stranger's nostrils flare. "There is an old poison in your blood," she says to Alanna.

"Yes." Alanna's cheeks flush, not entirely out of shame. "A being we call the Ancient One. I fought it, once, and survived. And I want to face it again, when I'm better armed."

"By all means," I say. The wind blows loud enough to drown out my voice. "You would find many allies, out there."

Alanna's eyes narrow. "You're not coming?"

A silence, as if before a storm.

I clench my fingers. Taste the old ripple of pain, the sky spinning drunken against the shell of my inner ear.

"Look at these hands," I say, and hold them out, two strange, wrinkled shapes of flesh. "Plasma shot from them, once. Imperial soldiers cowered at their raising. Would I parade myself, stripped of all armor, before those who only know of me from the stories, who shout themselves awake from nightmares of what I used to be? Would I give them my final humiliation?

"The war is over," I say, and heat leaks from my eyes again, surprising me. "And I am so, so tired."

For a full minute, Alanna and the pilot—and I can already see them together at the cockpit, cracking jokes, sipping the Starboard's famous green juice—stare, as if a viper has burst out of my mouth.

Then Alanna's fingers wrap around mine.

"You have made a home here," she says, low. "But are you staying because you want to, or because you're afraid?"

Dread climbs up my throat. That even in this body, I might be stripped of the few paltry defenses I have accumulated. That after all these years, I could be broken still further along these fractures I thought I knew.

"It's hard," Alanna says, and leaves gather on my tongue, and thorns. "It's so hard. I know."

Snowdrops bloom between our palms, at once binding her and pushing her away. Silent, I am a howl of green, a trampled husk, an empty room.

And afraid, down to my beating bones.

"Hedi," Alanna says, a murmur, a caress. "Hedi—"

And she is here, her thumb tracing the stems of the snowdrops, her other hand tremoring as it cups mine. She is here, and her eyes are a blade and a fire and a promise, and I don't know much anymore, but I know this: I will not go alone into the dark.

The pilot clears her throat. "I can, ah, give you some time," she ventures. "If you need to recalibrate—"

"No." I shake my head. Alanna's grip tightens, and I can taste the edge of her pulse, soft and round as a seed's first leaf. "I'm coming."

We step toward the ship, and Alanna's smile is like the sun.

Light Cone

TB Wright

Seth spooled down the near-C drives. The singular point of light in the infinite distance grew outwards, expanding into the speckled blackness of space. Mass returned to the vessel and Seth leaned forward in his chair, the well-worn leather creaking beneath his weight.

"Find Regal," he said. The computer began a scan of the night sky, pinpointing constellations and celestial bodies, triangulating Seth's position in the cosmos. Traveling close to the speed of light for so long meant astronomical drift and tiny miscalculations could add up to being millions of kilometers off course.

But he had been travelling the stars for longer than most could imagine, had set out into the dark out of a love for discovery and the great unknown. He knew what he was doing. Seth smiled when the computer came back with its results: right on target.

Not too bad.

A red dot lit up on his screen with the exact location of the settlement world of Regal.

Six years since he had last set foot on it. Over a century and a half to the inhabitants.

Relativistic time dilation was strange like that.

He tightened his jaw. Time to get this over with.

A few hours later, the blues and greens of the garden world materialized, a marble in the gloom. It had been little more than an outpost when Seth had left, maybe a few thousand people subsistence living, struggling to set up basic infrastructure before the colony ships arrived.

Now dozens of transponder signals blinked in orbit, a handful of habitation stations circling the planet. The capital city was just passing from the shade of night into the sun's glare, a blanket of lights spread out between two mountain ridges.

He scowled, chewed the inside of his cheek. Such a gaudy place. A sprawling metropolis on a largely undeveloped world in a back corner of settled space. Regal tried so hard to distinguish itself, set itself apart from other habitable planets. Even its name tried too hard! It was stupid coming back here. A huge waste of time.

Seth sighed. Unfortunately, if there was anything he had an abundance of, it was time.

After receiving docking orders, he descended to the city and found his assigned dock.

On the ground, the passage of time became even more apparent. Technologies, both recognizable and new, dotted the dockyard. He ordered repairs and a few upgrades from the dockmaster, hardly even glancing at their services. A week for the needed retrofit, then he would be gone again.

Using a public directory, he located the reason for his return and flagged down a taxi.

The city itself was a picture of modernity. Glistening scrapers into the sky. Sleek autotrams zipping about their multilayered rails. Peoples of all walks strolling clean, green streets, breathing fresh, unpolluted air.

The rampant growth of the colony, however, had spared the graveyard. Gravestone upon gravestone in a grassy field, non-indigenous trees providing shade from the high-altitude sun.

He hesitated before entering through the gates.

There was still time to abandon this pointless exercise. A week wasn't long to spend in some featureless hotel room, and that seemed more appealing than what waited for him here.

But no. He hadn't spent four years near the speed of light for nothing.

Jacob's grave was in the oldest part of the cemetery, nestled into the foothills of the mountains. A tree grew directly over it, casting a pleasant shade over the slab, wildflowers, ill-manicured grass.

Seth took one hesitant step after the next. Moss and weeds overgrew the marker. Seth clenched his jaw and knelt beside it, pulling at the moss and grass with his fingers, dirt embedding under his nails.

Gradually, he revealed the chiseled details.

Seth sat back. It was simple, just as Jacob would have wanted. His name, date of birth, date of death, a short epithet. Seth paid it no mind. He couldn't pull his eyes from the date of death.

Over a century ago, according to local clocks.

Jacob was long gone. Seth had known he would be, on an intellectual level, but now the force of it struck him. Based on the date, Jacob had lived most of his life after Seth had left.

Jacob had been bound to this world, anchored in time, missing out on so much of what Seth had seen. Events and people, discoveries and innovations that would have filled Jacob with joy and awe.

Instead, he was dead in the ground, long since decomposed back to the earth.

Seth forced his clenched fists open. Jacob had been an idiot for staying, but that had been his choice. He had made his desires clear.

It only took a few minutes kneeling in the grass to realize it had been a mistake coming back. What had Seth been looking for? Some sort of closure?

There was no closure here.

Seth pushed himself to his feet and glanced at the name one more time, his heart aching, and his blood boiling simultaneously. The week his ship would be in dry dock suddenly seemed an eternity.

He turned to find a man approaching with a quick gait, an anxious, almost awe-struck expression on his light tan face. He wore a tunic in a cut Seth didn't recognize and a satchel was slung over one shoulder, its contents bulging the fabric. The man stopped a few paces away, staring at Seth.

"Can I help you?" Seth said, his voice raw in his throat. He rubbed at his face, glanced at the wetness on his fingers. When had he started crying? He scrubbed the moisture away and turned up his chin towards this stranger.

"Are you...Seth Cosgrove?" the man asked, his voice quiet, reverent.

Seth narrowed his eyes.

The man quickly continued. "My name is Haythen. I'm, well, I guess you could say I'm an admirer of yours. I've been learning about the Relayers for years and figured you might come here one day. But to see you in the flesh..." He shook his head, a grin spreading on his face. "It's an honor to meet you."

Seth scowled. "The Relayers?"

Haythen beamed. "Oh, right! It's what I call all of you. It started as a relay race, right? Hence, Relayers."

That was the stupidest thing Seth had ever heard.

"I don't know who you are," Seth said, "but I'm leaving now."

"Wait," Haythen said, putting a hand up. "I would love to interview you. I've read so much about all of you, about your journeys and your exploits. Most people don't remember you, it was so long ago, but I do and I would love to know more."

Seth continued past Haythen. "I don't do interviews."

"Just a few questions," Haythen said, following him. "There's so much you've witnessed, so much you've been through! I want to share that with the world. We've forgotten so much of what you experienced firsthand."

"I'm not a teacher, I'm an explorer." Seth was almost at the gates, but he hadn't ordered a taxi yet. He cursed under his breath, snatched his pad from his pocket, and looked up a taxi service in the local directory. Luckily this backwater still followed the common standard and accepted Seth's currency.

Haythen circled around in front, walking backwards. "I can show you around the city. Anywhere you want to go, I know it. I've lived here my entire life."

"I'm sorry to hear it," Seth said, the veiled insult out of his mouth before he could stop it.

If Haythen registered it, he didn't let on. "Can you tell me about the Relayers? Why you all set off in the first place? Why you're the only one left?"

Seth sighed and dropped his shoulders, turning. He wasn't getting out of this, was he? "I'm the only one left because I'm the only one who kept my word. The only one who had the stomach for it, and the resolve to carry it through."

Haythen lit up. "Resolve to do what? There's so little information left from before the Scattering, I could never find why you all started hopping across time in the first place."

Seth screwed up his face. "We don't hop across time." He clenched his jaw and shook his head. This wasn't worth his time. "Why do you think I would tell you anything? They're all dead but me. Let them lie."

Seth stalked towards the entrance.

"And what about Jacob?"

Seth froze and slowly turned.

"Jacob died over a century ago. Why come back to his grave now?"

Seth licked his lips. He wanted to rage at this interloper. What business did he have digging into Jacob's life?

But Seth's own question resurfaced. Why had he come here?

"I won't press on anything personal," Haythen said, taking a few tentative steps closer, "but there's so much you know. So much you could share." He gave a disarming smile. "Just a few questions."

Seth chewed his lip, examining Haythen's face. His openness and gregariousness reminded him of the past. Of better times. When it had been just him and Jacob.

His finger hovered over his pad. He was already tired from this limited social interaction but...

Maybe it was nostalgia, or some pesky human desire to hear and be heard. He dropped his pad into his pocket.

"So how old are you?" Haythen asked.

At least he had had the courtesy to wait until Seth finished eating. "Of all your questions, that's the first?"

Haythen shrugged. "Like I said, records from before the Scattering are sparse. I couldn't find much on the Relayers. When were you born? *Where* were you born?"

Seth leaned back and glanced out the window onto the street beyond. Shadowed figures moved in flocks behind the tinted glass. "Earth," he finally said. "About twenty years before the Scattering began."

Haythen's eyes went wide. "You were there when it happened? Do you know *why* it happened?"

Seth shook his head. "We – the *Relayers*, though that's a dumb name – had already left. Your guess is as good as mine as to the cause of the Scattering. There was always some catastrophe or another. It seemed like we were going from one to the next every year. Maybe one was bigger than the rest, maybe multiple coincided and it was too much for Earth to handle." Seth shrugged. "All I know is that by the time we reached Alpha Centauri, it was over. Simple coincidence that our little jaunt into interstellar space and the collapse of Earth took place at the same time."

Haythen jotted down some notes, took an absent sip of juice. "How many Relayers were there at the beginning? How many made it to Alpha Cen?"

"Thirteen of us left Earth, only ten arrived. Space is dangerous, even more so back then. I could hazard a guess as to their fates." He sighed. "Thirteen people with more money than sense, wanting to go on an adventure, made a friendly wager: who could pass through one hundred years of relativity the fastest. You see, the faster you go, the closer you get to the speed of light, the more time passes for those on the ground. We wanted to see who could pass through one hundred relative years in the least amount of subjective time. With current propulsion, you could do it in five; five years in a ship going near-C, a hundred on Earth or Alpha Cen. Back then, it took longer. Only six of us made it to the one-hundred-year mark."

Haythen furrowed his brow. "So, you left Earth knowing that everyone you had ever known or loved, your family and friends, they would all be long dead by the time you reached Alpha Cen?"

"Of course," Haythen said, waving a hand. "We had each other; who else did we need? Generationally or independently wealthy, the best technology and know-how money could buy.

A small little club of the best and brightest, you could say." Seth smirked. "I think most of us were looking forward to passing the human race by."

Haythen examined him for a long moment before nodding slowly and jotting down more notes. "What happened to the other four Relayers? The ones that didn't reach one hundred years?"

"One or two of them died to accidents or malfunctions, though there's no way to tell for sure." Seth ran a finger through the perspiration on his drink. "But it turns out most of them simply weren't cut out for it. It became a chore for them and they dropped out." Seth rubbed the chill perspiration between his fingers. "I took it seriously."

"And Jacob?"

Seth glanced at him before looking away. "Jacob was like me. There was the adventure of it, but eventually that faded, and it simply became our way of life. A few months here, a few months there, interspersed with thirty, fifty, a hundred years of relative time in transit. It was exhilarating. Every time we exited near-C, there were new discoveries, new innovations. Centuries of human evolution. Everyone else died or gave up, but not us. Never us."

Why was he willingly offering his story? Haythen had no right to it. He should stop now, thank the man for lunch, and be on his way...but now that he had started, he found he didn't want to stop quite yet. The computer on his ship wasn't a great conversationalist, after all.

"But that didn't last." Haythen leaned forward, pushing aside his empty plate.

Seth's brow furrowed. "No. It didn't. We promised each other we would be in it for the long haul. This was our life, and we wouldn't stop. We would be together." He flicked a bead of moisture away. "But he broke his promise."

Haythen squinted. "That's it? Surely there was more to it than that? People don't break promises for no reason, especially after so long."

Seth scowled. "You want to know what happened?" He pointed out the window to the ever-present mountains surrounding the city. "We went up into the mountains, to one of our favorite spots, and he sprang it on me. We got into a fight. Things were said. I left."

"He wanted to stay, and you didn't?"

"He wanted to *quit*, and I didn't."

Haythen furrowed his brow. "But people change their minds, don't they? A few hundred years in near-C will wear on anyone."

Seth scowled, heat rising up his neck. "Jacob gave up on the journey and he gave up on us. It's that simple."

Haythen shook his head, a sad, almost pitying look in his eyes. "Promises have lifespans, regardless of the romantic ideals people have of them. People change. Just because he wanted something different from your itinerant lifestyle doesn't mean he gave up on you. He wasn't rejecting you. He was probably hoping you would embrace a fresh path with him."

Seth slammed a hand on the table, drawing the eyes of those seated around them.

Who was this stranger to question what happened? To question Jacob's mind? No one alive today had been there, had known either of them. A retort built in his throat, but he gritted his teeth and tamped it down.

All this talk of Jacob, of their last days together, was wearing on his soul, a deep exhaustion setting into his bones. Only forty-two years old, but at that moment he felt his full five hundred.

He pushed his chair back with a squeak and stood, making for the door.

Haythen followed behind silently.

There were too many people here, too much movement, too much sound and bluster. He leaned against a wall and rubbed his face.

A hand touched his shoulder, Haythen moving up beside him. Seth pulled away but regretted it. He was acting like a tantruming child.

"Are you okay?"

"It's too loud," Seth mumbled.

"I know a place we can go, away from all the crowds."

"Fuck you."

Haythen grimaced but kept on his shoulder. "It's quiet and secluded."

"I answered your inane questions already."

Haythen shrugged. "Do you have somewhere better to be?"

Unfortunately, he didn't. Despite his knack for hopping through time, he was powerless to speed up the drydock technicians.

"Fine. But no more questions."

Haythen led him up into the foothills overlooking the city. Seth caught his breath as the sounds of civilization faded. Birds in the air, the faint scent of wildflowers on the wind. It must be almost spring. He hadn't noticed.

Seth collapsed onto a bench on a bluff overlooking the valley.

"I never get tired of this view," Haythen said, sitting next to him.

The expanse of green and grey threatened to give Seth vertigo. There were no vistas like this in space. Endless distance in every direction and yet nothing to see most of the time.

"Why do you care so much?" Seth finally asked. "About me and Jacob, about the *Relayers*?"

Haythen thought for a long moment before answering.

"I studied to be a math teacher. I love numbers, I love teaching and I thought that would be my path. Then a few years ago I inherited some objects from my grandfather. At first, I thought they were just trinkets. Bobbles that he had hoarded away and now I had to go through and get rid of. But a few of them caught my eye. I investigated them further and before I knew it, I had fallen in love with their history. Developed a passion for finding out more. That led me to you and the Relayers. I had never heard of you before – I don't know if there are many who have, honestly. It's so far back in time and we know so little from those days. But once I started digging, I latched onto it." He glanced over at Seth. "I was hoping you would return to Regal one day."

Seth cocked his head. "Inherited objects?"

Haythen hesitated, licking his lip. "I must confess, I haven't been entirely truthful with you."

Seth lifted an eyebrow.

"I hadn't heard of you or the other Relayers, but I had heard of Jacob. He was my great grandfather."

Seth's breath caught in his throat, and he blinked.

"When my grandfather died a few years ago, some of Jacob's final effects passed to me. There had always been stories in our family about Jacob, but I never paid attention. Not until I started digging."

Seth didn't hear the rest of what Haythen said. His mind latched onto Haythen's last words and ran them in repeat.

Great grandfather.

Jacob had had a family. A partner, kids, grandkids. He hadn't only lived most of his life after Seth had left; he had *flourished*. Moved on. While Seth was still pining for someone long dead, Jacob had lived and loved, and his descendants were still around.

Seth shot to his feet, needing to move, needing to do anything but sit with the knot in his stomach. He paced to the edge of the bluff, scanning his eyes over the city below. How many down there had come from Jacob? Five? A dozen? More?

A line that had nothing to do with Seth, had no knowledge of what Seth and Jacob had shared.

Jacob had lived and loved here on Regal for the rest of his days.

Seth's chest tightened and a question burbled to the surface of his mind: what did *he* have?

The answer was clear.

Nothing.

Nothing but the stars and a life too long lived to be remembered.

"Are you okay?" Haythen asked, tentatively stepping towards him.

Seth backed away to the path and yanked his eyes from the view. "Don't follow me."

The sun was just passing into the shadows of the mountains when Seth found himself back at Jacob's grave. He had wandered for hours trying to clear his head, trying to dwell on anything but the sudden loneliness threatening to engulf him.

"I need to ask you something," he whispered to the silent cemetery. He rested a hand on the smooth stone of Jacob's marker. "I need to know that it meant something to you, like it did to me."

There was no answer.

Jacob was gone and had been for a century.

"Did you think about me before the end? Did you even remember my name?" He pressed his forehead against the cold stone. "At the beginning of this, we all set off with the understanding we didn't need the human race. We didn't need anyone. We had nothing to lose by passing through time in leaps and bounds." He shook his head. "But that wasn't true, was it? Not when I left you, and maybe it never was. We all had each other for a time and then it was just you and me. When did you decide it wasn't enough? Years before we came here? Or was it at that very moment when we crested the hill? You saw the valley and realized you wanted the earth instead of the stars. Did you think about me before you died, or was I just some faded memory?"

He shuffled over to the woody bark of the tree and collapsed against it.

His eyes wandered from the chiseled letters on Jacob's marker and for the first time, he registered the marker next to it. The matching epithets. The matching family names.

Jacob's husband, gone just a year before Jacob himself. They lived long lives together and as Seth's eyes roamed around the patch of long grass, more matching names stood out. Children, even some grandchildren, their own markers fanning out from Jacob's and his husband's at the center.

Generations come and gone and here Seth remained. Ageless in the eyes of his own species and entirely apart. Alone.

It could be him on the ground next to Jacob. This could be his kids and grandkids, but he had chosen the stars instead when all Jacob had wanted was a place to call home.

Was it possible to have it both ways? To have a place for yourself, for your loved ones, but also see everything there was to see, experience everything great swaths of time had to offer?

He sank into the hollow of the tree. The sun disappeared below the mountains.

Some time later, Haythen appeared from the gloom, illuminating his way with a flashlight. He approached slowly, somberly, and sat on the grass with a sigh.

"I'm sorry for any distress I caused. It wasn't my intent. I didn't know you and Jacob were so close."

Seth shrugged and waved away his concerns. "It's better to know than not, I suppose."

Haythen hesitated before pulling a yellowed paper envelope from his pocket. He unfolded it and handed it to Seth. "This was in Jacob's final possessions. I'm sorry to say I've already read it, but it led me to you, so I hope you'll forgive me."

Seth took the envelope in trembling fingers and held it up to Haythen's light.

*Seth,*it said on the front in Jacob's still-familiar, neat handwriting. Seth's breath caught, and he swallowed, opening the envelope, and withdrawing the single sheet of paper from within.

Seth, I hope one day you read this. I hope one day you return to Regal and I hope when you do you see its beauty the way I did.

I regret how we ended, but I do not regret my choice and I do not begrudge you yours. We were on the same path for a while and we grew together through it, but people change, and our changes were in opposite directions.

I wish we could have one more conversation. I want to know all the things you have seen and all the people you have met. But more than that I want to share with you the life I lived, in the hope you won't spend the rest of yours in the self-isolation you seem shackled to. You deserve more than what I was willing to give, as did I from you.

If you ever return to Regal I hope you think of me fondly as I still do of you daily.

Into the stars,

Jacob

Simple and to the point, just like the man himself. Not a declaration of undying love or regret for the life they could have had, but it was enough.

"I lied to you as well," Seth said into the cool stillness, clearing the emotion in his throat. "Jacob asked me to stay. Pleaded. But I've always had two loves: him, and that." Seth motioned towards the night sky, the stars mostly hidden by the light of the city. "I chose the latter, and now it's all I have left." He shook his head, brushed at the dot of liquid trickling down his face.

"Just because you've chosen a life out there doesn't mean you need to be alone and separate from the rest of us. There are worlds upon worlds out there, people in the trillions. You have knowledge of things they can't even dream of. You could share that with the rest of us and never be alone again." Haythen shrugged. "Who knows? Maybe one day you'll decide that you've had enough as well. Everyone's journey is unique. What worked for him doesn't need to be your path."

Seth nodded, his heart a bit lighter with Jacob's letter in his hand. "I don't know how to teach," he said with a bitter laugh. "I hardly even know how to live anymore."

Haythen cracked a grin. "You know, I trained to be a teacher."

Seth cocked his head before his eyes went wide with Haythen's meaning. "But this is your home. You've lived here your entire life."

"And I'm ready to see what's out there."

"You would likely never return, at least not in the lifetimes of your family, of everyone you know."

Haythen nodded. "I know. They do as well. I was going to leave sooner or later, regardless."

"Thirteen of us set out from Earth all those centuries ago, and now there's only me. What makes you think you'll be able to stand it?"

Haythen shrugged. "Maybe I won't, but just because we choose something today doesn't mean we need to choose it tomorrow, right?"

Seth examined Haythen in the gloom. Now that he knew what to look for, the ghost of Jacob's features was unmistakable.

Could Seth travel with someone again, with the knowledge that it might end suddenly and abruptly, just like last time?

The answer dawned on him gently: he had never once regretted the time Jacob and he had spent together, despite its tumultuous conclusion. Maybe it was time for Seth to rejoin society, even if in this small way. And after all, if there was anything he had an abundance of, it was time.

Seth nodded. "Alright."

How Far the Ocean Goes

Lillian Barry

Every morning the sun put its shiny fingers on the edge of the Ocean and peeked up to see if Jouey was awake.

Jouey usually *was* awake, curled up in their wings at the mouth of their cave on the Mountain. But they were not interested in the sun personally—their interest was more, well, intellectual, no offence intended—so they did not return the sun's overtures of friendship.

A calculator by profession, Jouey knew the sun must be some measurable, empirical distance away. And they knew the edge of the Ocean lay somewhere along that distance, in the same way that if you looked down a stick of celery and put your palm at the end of it, you knew there was no celery beyond your hand. The celery was a finite length. Ergo, there must be a measurable, empirical answer to their question: How far does the Ocean go?

"Will you please stop asking me that question?" said Nerine, the rival calculator who lived in the Valley under the Mountain.

"I'll stop asking when you can answer it," returned Jouey. "And until you can, I'll still be the finest calculator in all the Isles."

"I bet *you* don't even know how far the Ocean goes."

Jouey didn't. As a winged person with an above average wingspan (they had calculated), they'd tried to fly across the Ocean many times. But it went on and on, and the horizon kept glistening and glinting and never coming closer, and they always ran out of stamina before they reached it. The Ocean was farther than they could fly and bigger than they could calculate. And shinier and more enticing than their desire could bear.

"Now leave me alone, I have *actual* clients here with *actual* problems."

Nerine flipped her glossy, sun-bleached hair. She'd never understand. She was a land person, a legs person—oh, but those *legs*, though—wingless and without Jouey's ache to know the impossible. Sometimes Jouey resented their wings; wings made them ambitious enough to fly for the horizon, when it would be easier to plant their feet firmly on the land. Still, that was only speculation. They wished they knew (another impossible) what Nerine was really thinking and feeling under that beautiful hairy halo of hers.

Jouey left Nerine puzzling with the milkman over how many cows he should count to fall asleep at night, and took the path back to the road, where they ran their mobile calculator service. They didn't really travel these days—it was more fun setting up camp near Nerine's cottage and sniping her less loyal customers—but "mobile" was a buzzword in small business branding. Customers wanted you to be willing to come to them, even though, in reality, people came to see Nerine (and therefore Jouey) from all over.

Here was one, in fact. The rumble of horses' hooves, along with an unidentifiable scraping sound like a giant piece of sandpaper grazing a cliffside, made Jouey glad Nerine had shooed them away. A customer with a horse probably had deep pockets. Well worth ripping off.

Jouey spread their feathered cloak on the ground and had just enough time to arrange their pebbles and sticks—tools of the calculating trade—before a riderless horse pulled up with a huff and a whinny. It dragged a wooden dinghy, ostensibly the source of the scraping sound.

"Bleeding hot," said the horse. "I know you don't have oceans in the countryside, but do you happen to know any lakes? Tarns? Lochs? Ponds? I'll take a puddle."

"Are you looking for a drink or a bath?" asked Jouey.

"Blowed if I know," said the horse. "You can't drink the Ocean, mind you—the Salty Stallion made sure of that, back when the giants were serving it as soup at their dinner parties and the reefs started drying up. I'm just so damn *thirsty.*"

Jouey had never met a seahorse before, but, judging by the gills on its flanks and the fluttering fins on its hooves, this new acquaintance was one of them.

"I have something better than a puddle," they said, untying the skin from their belt. "Here."

The horse glugged the skin greedily, then its eyes rolled back and it collapsed on the road. As it went down it yanked the ropes attached to its bridle and the dinghy jumped a foot in the air.

"Gruuugh," came a voice.

A red-coated stranger sat up in the dinghy and rubbed his eyes. He took in the unconscious horse and Jouey sitting on their cloak nearby.

"And what hath come to pass?" he intoned in a deep, pampered accent.

Aha. Here was the person with the deep pockets.

"I gave him a drink," said Jouey with a shrug.

"Of what, pray?" asked the stranger suspiciously.

"Lemonade. He drank my whole supply for the day, so you owe me."

"Ha!" laughed the stranger. "And how, verily, do you figure I, a simple traveller, will pay you?"

"From the enormous pouch on your belt," said Jouey. "Besides, you must be very rich to be wearing a red coat like that. You must be a king. Only kings wear red."

"Barnacles," swore the stranger, dropping the accent. He spoke quite normally now. "I'm only a prince, though. Haven't passed the king exam yet."

"I am a calculator and a tutor available for hire," said Jouey equably, holding their hand out. "You can see I am very good at figuring."

The prince did not touch their hand. "You're the calculator I was sent to find? The finest calculator in all the Isles?"

"Most certainly," boasted Jouey. "Test me."

"Alright. How many gold coins do I have in my pouch?"

Jouey's stomach gurgled at the vision of gold hiding inside that impermeable leather. They breathed deep, kept their brain level, and twitched their outstretched hand. The prince sighed, but amenably reached into his pouch and brought out a coin to drop into their palm.

The coin shone in their hand. It told them its memories, and Jouey knew how many coins were in the pouch.

"Fifty-six coins, excluding this one," they said.

The prince sighed again, and cast an eye over the spread of rocks and sticks on their cloak. "I suppose you must be a calculator," he said. "You are not what I expected, from your mother's account."

Jouey jolted out of their complacency at having secured another of Nerine's customers. "My mother?" they asked. They had never met their mother.

"Yes, the boatbuilder who lives on the far side of the Bay," said the prince. "She told me where to find you."

The unfamiliar burn of shame clawed up Jouey's throat. They knew Nerine had left her home in the Bay; they knew, even without asking, that Nerine missed her mother, by the way she sucked the single pearl on her string necklace between her lips whenever she was working on a particularly difficult problem.

"Well, perhaps I am not the person you're looking for," they said slowly, though it killed them to give up this customer and his fifty-six gold coins, "but I *am* a calculator."

The prince tilted his head in question.

"Another calculator lives in the cottage down the road," said Jouey. "Nerine. She comes from the Bay."

"Ah, then I'll go to Nerine," said the prince.

As he turned away, his pouch swung in a wide circle, carried by its weighty contents. Desperation tugged at Jouey's tongue.

"She is my colleague," they added. "We work together."

A neat lie, they thought. And not wholly untrue, since they were really doing Nerine a favour.

The prince threw a smile over his shoulder. "Then you'd better come with me!"

Nerine did not look best impressed when Jouey followed the prince into her spotless home, the tips of their wings grazing the brass pots and pans hanging on the walls. But she looked more confused than anything when the prince called Jouey her "colleague."

"I am so lucky they brought me to you," he said, beaming. "What a rare day it is to find who you're looking for!"

Jouey smirked at Nerine's questioning glance; they knew she was far too proper to argue in public.

"So, what's the problem?" Nerine asked with a small sigh. She probably had a full day of business to attend to, and she would never fob off the village folk for a fancy client.

"Ah, well, it is quite distressing. If it's not too much to ask, could I give you a smaller problem first?"

Nerine sniffed. Jouey could tell she found the request insulting. "I would be happy to leave the task to Jouey," she said. Nerine's pride would not let gold be her motive, not like Jouey, when she could get almost everything she needed from the villagers in exchange for her services. So predictable.

The prince's face fell. "Oh, but I really wanted to hire you. Your mother spoke so highly of you."

Nerine froze. Her lips went white, her nose pinched and frostbitten. "My mother?" she prompted.

"Yes, yes, the reason we're all here," Jouey groused. Otherwise they'd have taken the job themself and never breathed Nerine's name. Come to think of it, they weren't entirely sure why they hadn't done that. "Your mother told this fancy fella you're the finest calculator in the Isles. Which, by the way, is not true. I solved his little test in a heartbeat."

"I don't need to compete," said Nerine.

"And this is why *I'm* the finest calculator."

"You can believe what you like."

"You're no fun."

The prince watched this exchange with a tug of his lips. "You would be doing me a favour, Ms Nerine, if you could tell me how many coins I have here in my pouch. So I can be sure no scallywags sleighted any from me on my way to your door."

Scallywag? Jouey preferred "unethical businessperson."

They suppressed a cough as Nerine's side-eye caught them by the throat. They swallowed and shrugged, leaving Nerine to snatch the pouch and place it on her scales. She began to pile pebbles from her collection onto the counterbalance, adjusting every now and then. At length she turned around.

"Fifty-eight coins," she said.

Nearly, Jouey thought.

The prince beamed once again. "Well, I'm blessed," he exclaimed. "Two extremely fine calculators in the same town."

Jouey grinned. This just proved the prince didn't have a clue how many coins he had. That was fine; fifty-six and fifty-eight were the same to most people—and indeed, rich people themselves did not need to know how to count.

"I simply must hire you both," he said. "Two heads are better than one, isn't that what they always say?"

Jouey wasn't sure about that.

"I am rather busy." Nerine nibbled on her nails, the way she did when she was agitated. "I would rather know the problem before accepting the job."

"Yes, of course." And the prince flounced into the only armchair in the place and steepled his hands. "You see, my kingdom has recently been attacked. There is a monster on the loose. A sea monster. The kingdom will be destroyed if we do not act."

Sea monsters did not bother Jouey, who lived on the Mountain and worked in the Valley, but they didn't miss Nerine's sharp gasp. They supposed sea monsters must be the bane of a seaside kingdom.

"I am raising an army to subdue the monster," said the prince, "but we have lost so many soldiers already, it has been troubling me...how many soldiers will I need to defeat the monster?"

Jouey was immediately intrigued. And so, by the determined crease of Nerine's brow, was she.

"That is a vague question," Nerine remarked. "We will need to know a lot more about your army, and your weapons, and most importantly about the monster itself."

"And I will tell you everything I can," said the prince, "before I have to get back to my garrison tomorrow. But will you take the task? Can you solve the problem?"

"Yes," said Nerine emphatically at the same time as Jouey said, "With enjoyment, and half the fee upfront."

Nerine glowered at them, but the prince good-naturedly paid up thirty of his fifty-six gold coins, and Nerine served elbowroot tea while the two of them quizzed him for the particulars.

When he finally left to retrieve his horse (rousing now from its lemonade-induced stupor) and return to his kingdom, Nerine rounded on Jouey.

"Why?" she demanded.

"The money, of course." Jouey jingled the sixteen gold coins now stuffed into their parched waterskin.

"That's not what I meant," Nerine said.

Jouey knew all too well what she meant, but all they said was, "We'll make time to meet up and start work on this." And they whistled themself out the door and took off up towards the Mountain. And if they felt Nerine's curious gaze on the sensitive area between their shoulderblades where their wings grew, it couldn't make them shiver in the day's heat, not really.

The next morning, the sun shook its golden tresses across the water, but nobody was there to see it. The morning after, its flirtations again went unseen, and by the third day, the sun rose glaring at the cave mouth in the Mountain where Jouey usually sat.

But Jouey wasn't there. Jouey had found themself sleeping on the other side of the Mountain, looking over the Valley and watching for the lamp in Nerine's cottage to wink on in the morning. That was their signal, they had decided, to fly down and bother the rival calculator. And oddly enough, Nerine let them in, and they worked on the prince's problem together.

Jouey had never calculated with another person before, but they found they enjoyed it. The theory felt more robust with another person to bounce ideas off and keep track of all the paths of logic. They liked when Nerine gave a soft nod of approval or assent to their insights, and even liked when Nerine's insights elicited that same nod from them.

On the fourth day, they met at the waterfall in the Valley. Jouey was early. The sun had not yet crested the Mountain and the shallow ravine lay in shadow, gnats dancing over the still pools at the riverside. A common garden gnome perched on the bank eating his breakfast, and Jouey tried not to stare as he ate his porridge and thereafter ate his bowl.

"Hungry?" Nerine asked.

The earth had told Jouey of her footsteps long before she came up and touched their shoulder, but the warm pressure of her fingertips still made them startle.

"Ha," they said, unexpectedly breathless. They were not used to being surprised. It was easier to predict that something would happen than how they would feel when it did.

Their feathers quivered as Nerine twirled a basket of glowberries under their nose.

"Oh, you really were asking if I was hungry."

The berries gleamed in the basket, and Jouey popped one in their mouth without asking. Juice exploded over their tongue and they let out a groan.

"Well, there's my answer," Nerine murmured as if to herself.

She was gazing at them, lips stained with berry juice already and slightly parted. Something peculiar stirred in Jouey's gut.

"Shall we get to work?" they suggested, shaking themself.

They squatted at the water's edge to study the tiny waterbeasts that were born in the reeds. Most of them got eaten before they made it to the Ocean and grew to become gigantic, unkillable sea monsters. Well, Nerine hoped they were not unkillable. Jouey had their doubts, but all they knew from their work so far was that it would take an awful lot of soldiers to bring down the beast tearing the seaside kingdom apart.

Even with two calculators on the case, Jouey had not had to work this hard in a while. In their day-to-day dealings they were able to rely for the most part on their gift of prediction. Gamblers would've called it game sense; storytellers called it plot armour and mystics called it premonition. Such a skill was less acceptable in the profession of a calculator, although Jouey's version of that employed elements of gambling and storytelling and mysticism alike. But in their honest attempt at a serious problem, it was difficult to hide how, exactly, they knew how many ingots of steel it took to make a standard issue military spear from the seaside kingdom.

"You have it, don't you?" asked Nerine.

"I have many things," returned Jouey.

"But not money, apparently."

Jouey, who lay on the bank while Nerine waded in the river, pushed up on their elbows and frowned. "What do you mean?"

"Isn't that the reason you took the job? I know how you gaze at gold. But what do you need money for? You live on the Mountain and the winged people are self-sufficient."

The sun had risen now and its ripples on the water dappled Nerine's ankles enticingly. The waterbeasts nipped at the tiny hairs on her skin that caught the light.

"I like shiny things," Jouey explained simply.

Nerine's laughter pealed through the ravine. It was a lovely sound, but it tore at a part of Jouey's heart that had always been empty. They reached for the basket of berries to fill it.

"What about you?" they asked. "Why did you take the job?"

Nerine's laughter faded. "I want to save the world."

Jouey could have laughed in return, but they didn't. "Your mother lives on the far side of the Bay," they said. "You care about her."

Nerine ducked her head to nibble at the pearl around her neck. "Sometimes it's hard not to," she said on a breath.

Jouey could've asked why she wouldn't care. But they understood enough. Family was complicated. "She sent the prince to find you."

"Mm. The prince said she told him I'm the finest calculator in all the Isles." Nerine smiled, something like hope peeking out from under her eyelashes.

"Well, we both know that's not true."

Their eyes met and they both laughed.

⸺◈⸺

By evening, they were tired and grouchy. Their research had gone well, but the calculation had not.

"Something's wrong," Jouey grumbled. "We're not asking the right question."

"Then what question should we be asking?"

"I don't know. But doesn't something feel amiss to you?"

Nerine chewed their pearl. "No."

It was a lie. Her eyes told Jouey so.

In hunger and frustration, Jouey turned their back and stomped up the bank. Suddenly the ground crumbled under their angry feet. They slipped. They could have flown out of danger, but, longing to feel an impact, they let themself fall. They tumbled into the deep part of the river, up to their chest in icy water. It shocked the frustration right out of them.

Then they realised their mistake.

A thousand miniscule waterbeasts swarmed from the reeds and with their wings drenched Jouey struggled to propel themself back to the bank. By the time they were back on dry land, a gaping hole had been eaten in their shirt.

Nerine, who had watched the whole thing with her hands covering a giggle, gasped.

Jouey looked down at the hole. Blast it. Of course the waterbeasts had made a hole *there*. They, like Jouey, were drawn to shiny things. Now Nerine was staring in horror at the patch of reddish scales on their torso.

They took off their wet, useless shirt and waited for Nerine to say something.

"Is that a conflict of interest?" she said eventually.

"What?"

"We're supposed to be figuring out how to defeat a sea monster."

Jouey barked out a laugh. "Maybe. But I don't want to see a town destroyed any more than you do. Though it really is mostly for the gold."

"You weren't lying when you said you like shiny things."

Jouey nodded and found they were content with Nerine's reaction. "You asked what I need money for. Well, it's for my hoard."

It was an absurd admission to a land person like Nerine who used gold to pay the thatcher to fix her roof. Then again, she had her own hoard of sorts: she collected pebbles, and only mostly for her job. She'd pocketed a few from the river just today, if she saw a shape she liked or a pretty marbling.

"But why gold?" she asked.

"Because it's shiny."

"Loads of things are shiny."

"Ah, yes, let me put the Ocean in a bottle and bring it to my dark cave." The Ocean was sparklingly desirable; they wanted to know how far the Ocean went but that didn't mean they thought they could keep it for themself.

Nerine shook her head. "I can show you something better than gold. Cheaper than money."

"You can?"

"Yes. I'll take you there tomorrow."

Jouey shook the water off their wings. Knowing what a strenuous flight it would be up the Mountain, damp and hungry, they accepted Nerine's offer to go back to her cottage and share bread and stew and bed on the floor beside the fire.

It was strange to wake up the next morning in the cold stone cottage, the sun nowhere to be seen, though its rays curled around the Mountain in search of Jouey. Nerine showed them how to cook eggs on the hearth and they set out on the path that wound round the Mountain. It would be quicker to fly, of course, but that would be rude.

The Ocean sparkled into view shortly before midday, and Jouey breathed a contented sigh. The Mountain jutted out from the land, the Bay curving around the Ocean in a wide embrace. The seaside kingdom was in the middle of the Bay, and Nerine, Jouey knew, was from the very far side of the Bay, almost as far as the eye could see.

"Where are you taking me?" Jouey asked for the hundredth time. "I live on the Mountain. You can't show me anything I haven't seen before."

Nerine smiled and kept walking.

Eventually they reached a dark inlet under the Mountain. Jouey had never been there before, but they weren't going to admit that. The low spring tide had exposed a plain of craggy granite dotted with rockpools.

"Are we going fishing?" they asked.

"Jouey! You never say that."

"You never say 'I'm going fishing'?"

"Shush! You say 'I'm going out to sea.' Otherwise the fish might hear you."

"Fish don't have ears."

"But the Ocean does."

Nerine glared at Jouey till they shrugged their agreement. She'd grown up by the sea and her mother built boats for the fisherpeople; she knew things they didn't.

Nerine twisted her skirt and tucked it inside her belt. "Now. Are you ready? I'm going to need your help."

Jouey nodded, although they didn't know what for.

They followed her into the warm pools and helped her overturn a boulder, then put it back, then another boulder, then put it back. Nerine sucked her pearl; she must be calculating. Jouey watched a loose end of her skirt swirling in the shallow water, exposing every now and then the shape of her leg.

A cry of victory brought their eyes back up. Nerine pointed at the rock she'd just turned.

"What?" asked Jouey, seeing nothing.

"Look closer."

Wet brown granite. A clump of seaweed. Stripy, conic limpet shells. Open mouth of a dead fish abandoned by the tide. Scuttling legs as a small crab found a new hiding place. Closer. Tiny white barnacles clinging to the rock. Streaks of discolouration from old seaweeds and corals. Little pinprick holes. Wait. Closer. The arc of holes decorated a lump on the rock which was perhaps a shade greyer, a grade finer, than everything else.

Jouey turned a questioning glance on Nerine, whose pink mouth broke into a smile. She took her knife from her pouch and pried the lump from the rock. It came away with a scratch and a pop, and Jouey recognised it as some kind of mollusc.

"What is it?" they asked.

"An ormer." Nerine dropped it into her pouch and peered into a crevice in the rockpool.

"But why?" It was wholly unclear to Jouey why Nerine had brought them here. Weren't they looking for something better than gold? What had this ugly grey sea snail to do with their need for shiny things? "What do you do with them?"

"You eat them. Here. Let's find a second one, then we can both have one."

Jouey was hungry, so they helped Nerine look. Together they spotted a few more, but Nerine made them leave the smaller ones safe under the rocks where they found them, until they finally found another ormer the size of a handspan.

"No more than one each," said Nerine firmly. "There aren't many of them. Besides, collecting stops being fun if you collect too fast. We can take one ormer each per visit."

Jouey had no idea why Nerine thought they'd want to collect ormers, but they bit their tongue till they'd returned to the shore and dried their feet on the grass.

"So can we eat now?" they asked.

Nerine's laugh echoed against the cliffs. "We have to get back to my cottage and cook them first."

Was she serious? The sun was past its zenith and Jouey hated being hungry.

"I have a better idea," they said. "My cave has an entrance on this side of the Mountain. It would be so much quicker to go there and cook them."

"Your cave on the Mountain? How am I supposed to get up there? I'm no climber."

She could be so unimaginative.

"I'll take you. If you'll let me."

Jouey wiggled their fingers. Nerine's throat bobbed as she swallowed, then nodded. They stepped closer, and closer again, and wrapped their fingers round her waist from behind. Oh. Oh dear. She was warm and firm and her hair smelled of calyptus as it tickled their neck. Maybe this was not such a good idea.

"Are you sure you can carry me?" Her breath slipped through the sea air and painted patches of heat on Jouey's cheeks.

"Of course I can. You know I could've moved all those rocks for you earlier."

"Then why didn't you?"

An excellent question. Jouey knew it was because they enjoyed doing it together, in the same way as they liked working on the prince's calculation together.

Rather than admit it, though, they spread their wings and sprang into the air. Nerine yelped as her body dropped under theirs, but they held her tightly, and her yelps turned into whoops as the ground grew further away. Jouey couldn't see her face, but they felt her elation in the seizures of her diaphragm as she cried for joy at flying for the first time.

They grinned, and took her up the Mountain.

⁕

Jouey lit the fire while Nerine enjoyed the view. She'd been quiet since Jouey had set her back on solid land, but when they asked if she was alright, she just gave a shy smile that stilled their questions even as it stoked their curiosity.

Once the fire was hot, Nerine dug the ormers out of their shells with her knife, removing the chewy bits, scrubbed the slime off the foot, and pounded them till flat and white and tender. Jouey ate mostly nuts and berries and whatever they could forage, so they didn't keep much in the way of bought or processed goods, but they did have flour and seasoning, and

Nerine made a simple crumb before frying the ormers off in the fire.

They ate them with seaweed they'd found in the rockpool and roasted root vegetables from Jouey's reserves.

"They're good," said Jouey as they crunched on the tough, salty meat, "but I still don't understand why they're better than gold."

Nerine chuckled. "It's not about the food." She reached for the shells she'd discarded during the prep and scraped the guts out with her knife. "Here."

Jouey inspected the shell she held out. It was still dull on the outside, but on the inside, where the ormer had been, it shone. Their heart leapt. A pearlescent sheen glowed in the firelight, patterned and pleasantly textured as the light seemed to swirl into the well of the shell and pool in the arc of holes on the edge they'd noticed before.

"It's beautiful," they breathed.

"Turn it to the sun," said Nerine.

Jouey took it to the mouth of the cave. The sun was on the other side of the Mountain now, so they had to go further to catch its light. But when they did, a whole rainbow appeared, all purples and greens and blues in hues they'd never imagined possible.

"Do you like it?" asked Nerine, gazing at their face.

Jouey found they couldn't hide their pleasure even if they wanted to. "It's everything I like best about shiny things and more."

"Is it better than gold?"

They huffed a laugh. "Maybe." It was certainly better than gold. Gold was shiny, yes, but it had a flat palette, nothing like the ripple of colours in this shell, and it didn't have the fascinating spiral shape, either. They might even consider getting rid of the hoard of gold that they'd stashed in a secret tunnel in the Mountain.

They didn't tell Nerine that, but they were overcome by the urge to open up to her.

"Look at the Ocean," they said. "That's what I like best. The sun on the waves. Always moving. Always seething. Beckoning you over. But where, you don't know."

"Is that why you're always asking how far the Ocean goes? You want to know where the light leads?"

Jouey had to screw their eyes shut against the mortal experience of being seen for the first time. "I know it's just a reflection of the sunlight," they said.

"But you're drawn to it."

"Yes."

They gazed at each other, then back out at the Ocean, and a silence settled over their shared contemplation of the horizon. When Jouey looked back at Nerine, a twist of sadness had pulled her mouth out of its usual smile.

"What's up?" they asked softly.

"I was thinking about my mother," Nerine confessed.

"What about her?"

"My mother taught me how to find shiny shells," Nerine explained. "I grew up with the fisherpeople and the oyster farmers. That's where I learned to calculate: figuring out the ormer stocks and the oyster yields for the season. Knowing when to stop collecting to ensure the sustainability of the species. I loved it."

"Then why did you leave?" It was something Jouey had often wondered.

"My mother. I didn't want to see her any more. But I know she misses me, and I worry about her. I hope she knows I'm well and happy. Even if I'm...not the kind of happy she envisioned for me."

To most land people, Nerine's feelings might have seemed confusing or contradictory. They made perfect sense to Jouey, who'd deliberately chosen a secluded part of the Mountain to make their home away from the majority of their community. They were a loner, yes, but there were reasons for that. It was hard to enjoy being around people who did not see you for who you were.

"How would you feel about sending your mother a gift?" they asked, keeping their voice light and even.

Nerine looked up in surprise. "What kind of gift?"

Jouey gestured to the clump of nerine sarniensis, the local lily, flowering above the mouth of their cave. "Does she have a garden?"

"Would she know it was from me?" whispered Nerine as if afraid of the answer.

"Only one way to find out."

"But she lives on the other side of the Bay."

"Well, how did you like flying with me?"

Nerine's face flushed as scarlet as the flower itself. "I liked it very much."

"Then shall we do it again?" Jouey could hardly hear their own voice over the pounding of their heart. But when they reached out to their rival, colleague, and now, maybe, friend, her slender fingers slipped easily into theirs.

"I'd love to," she said.

Now it was Jouey's second time with their hands on her body, they let themself feel and adjust for the best purchase. She was so soft under her dress. They chose the strongest, firmest part of her, that would let her hang perfectly balanced against their wingbeats and the air resistance as they soared across the Bay.

And that was what they did, with the water far below and the salt stinging their eyes. Nerine gulped up the air and threw her arms out like Jouey's wings, making them both giggle. The seaside kingdom stretched between the land and the sea, busy and bustling, with the makeshift barracks on the sand where the prince was raising his army, and a few smoking buildings that must have been destroyed by the monster recently. Jouey ignored both the sight and the twinge to their conscience, keeping their resolve on the purple hills in the distance and the fishing village on the cape.

They landed on what Nerine called the Common, an expanse of grazing land. It was easy to hide among the clumps of yellow gorse and bracken while the sun completed its arc over the land and the air began to cool and darken with evening.

At twilight, Nerine led the way to the fishing village on the edge of the Common, but she hung back after pointing out her mother's cottage.

"I don't want her to see me."

"Then she won't," Jouey promised. "You wait here. I've got this."

Leaving Nerine in the shadow of the village well, Jouey crept to the front of the whitewashed cottage. With their long nails they scooped a small hole in the earth and dropped a lily seed into the crack. They covered it up and sprinkled some water from their skin. Then they took their new ormer shell from their belt and carefully reflected moonlight and rainbows onto the damp patch. They could feel it, they could feel the seed crying out to grow, and they coaxed it up through the earth and into the open. A stem, a bud, and finally a flower.

"Jouey!" Nerine gasped a warning, and Jouey grabbed their shell and dived into the shadow of the well.

A weathered woman emerged from the cottage, the door creaking behind her. She bent to the pile of firewood under the porch, but stopped when she saw the flower outside her house. It was wild and red and out of place in the moonlit village.

But her cracked face split into tears as she knelt beside the flower and touched the velvety petals. "Nerine," she wept.

And Nerine, close enough to watch but far enough not to be heard, was weeping too. "That's the first time she's called me by my name," she cried.

Jouey offered their shoulder and let her sob into the nook. "Is that why you didn't want to see her?" they asked.

"Yes." Nerine sniffed and watched her mother dry her tears in her apron and shuffle back into the cottage. "Maybe I would see her now."

"You don't have to."

"I'm just glad she knows I'm okay."

But before Jouey could reply, an almighty snort sounded from the Ocean, and a gigantic shape rose half a mile in the water to block out the moon. Six silver eyes made nothing of the distance between itself and Jouey, and it lunged, its humongous body crashing over the Common and making the grazing flocks wail and flee.

"Is it looking at us?" Nerine shook in Jouey's arms.

"It's okay, it can't reach us here," said Jouey, projecting more confidence than they felt. The beast had clearly not revealed its full size.

"Can it reach the village?"

"Maybe if it comes round the headland."

"Then we have to lead it away!" she cried. "Please! We have to save my mother!"

"I don't think it wants your mother." Then what did it want? Jouey asked themself. They weren't sure. Not yet. They touched the ground, trying to find the rock beneath, and the water, and thereafter the beast itself, but the beast wouldn't show them its stories. They could not predict what did not want to be known.

The monster reared again, this time closer, around the headland. Its scales glistened in the moonlight and Jouey swallowed the sick feeling of irrepressible desire in their gut that wouldn't leave them despite the terror of the creature.

"We have to go," they said, catching Nerine in their arms and taking off as the beast swung its body again down on the land.

It screeched in protest as they climbed the air till it looked like nothing more than a scaly worm writhing in a puddle.

"Did we bring it here?" Nerine quavered.

"No, it's been terrorising the Bay for a while, the prince said."

Nerine crumpled in Jouey's arms, offsetting their balance and causing them to swerve. The monster was undulating towards the seaside kingdom now, wailing with rage.

"We've been distracted," Nerine said. "We were supposed to figure out how many soldiers the prince needs. Are we too late?"

"I still think we're asking the wrong question."

Jouey frowned into the darkness. What did the monster really want? They tried to recall the scene of the two of them crouching behind the well when the monster had appeared. Think! The flower in the garden. The roof of the well. The ormer shell glinting on the ground where they'd dropped it to hold Nerine as she cried.

The shell. Its shining rainbows. Glinting in the moonlight.

Jouey had to test their theory. They flew in the monster's wake towards the seaside kingdom, nearing the barracks in time to watch the beast sweep a claw through an entire squadron. It lifted the screaming soldiers to its mouth, crunched down on their swords and spat away the bodies. The soldiers crawled away, cowering, crushed but alive.

That was it.

Jouey scanned the sea wall for the prince, and found him relaying orders to his captains. They swooped close, till he looked up and his expression hardened.

"You didn't solve the problem!" yelled the prince. "You left it too late!"

Jouey knew they weren't getting their money now, but the gold didn't matter any more. Not with the ormer shell in their belt and Nerine in their arms.

"You don't need soldiers!" they called back. "Give the monster all your weapons and armour!"

The prince looked incredulous for a second, then folded his arms across his heirloom breastplate.

Another watery snort ripped from the Ocean. The monster had found them. It had almost certainly seen the prince, whose armour was the prettiest and shiniest of them all.

"Quickly!" yelled Jouey, and Nerine, catching on, urged him the same.

With the monster raising its enormous head, poised to strike, the prince clearly saw his life in the balance with no better ideas, and he stripped off his armour and legged it just in time. The beast crashed down on the wall, leaving a gaping wreckage where the prince had stood. It balanced the prince's breastplate in its jaws and disappeared into the water for an instant before reappearing empty-mouthed.

"It has dragon blood, all it wants is shiny things," Jouey called down to the drenched, shivering prince.

"Well, why didn't you say so before?"

The prince barked some orders along the walls and his soldiers began to build a pile of weapons and armour on the beach. The monster reared one more time and the fury had faded from its eyes as it began to pluck piece after piece from the pile and swallow it into the Ocean. It ignored the soldiers, the prince, and Nerine and Jouey.

When the pile was gone, the monster finally vanished with a flick of its tail and a shower of spray.

The prince was panting heavily. "I owe you," he said, pulling the leather pouch from his belt.

Jouey could hear the coins jingling inside, but they no longer desired them.

They shook their head. "Keep the gold," they said. "If the monster comes back, you'll need something shiny to give it."

The prince winced. "Will it come back?"

"Who knows? But if it does, now you know what it wants. A collection."

Nerine chuckled, and Jouey caught her twinkling eye. They smiled at each other.

"We'd better go home," Jouey said. "It's been a long night."

The prince groaned. "I'll say."

"Good luck with the king exams," said Jouey, and together with Nerine, they took off back towards the Mountain.

"How did you know?" asked Nerine.

"Usually I ask my surroundings," said Jouey, "but this time I asked myself. I suppose I have something in common with the sea monster."

"It's hard to calculate something unless you're familiar with it," said Nerine.

She swivelled her gaze to the open sea, where the sun was putting its golden fingers on the edge of the Ocean to see if Jouey was awake.

"You're very practical," commented Jouey.

"Mm, well. I had another practical thought...if you want to know how far the Ocean goes, how about we find out? We can measure it. Maybe my mother would lend us a boat."

The vice of adrenaline that had been squeezing Jouey's insides all night relaxed, and something else swelled there that they'd never felt before.

"You'd ask your mother for a boat?"

"Can't know what she'll say until we ask."

And that's how the finest calculator in all the Isles, and her winged lover, set off together to find out how far the Ocean goes.

THE AUTHORS
IN ORDER OF APPEARANCE

GABRIELLA BUBA

Gabriella is a mixed Filipina writer and chemical engineer based in Texas who likes to keep explosive pyrophoric materials safely contained in pressure vessels or between the covers of her books. She writes adult romantic fantasy for bold, bi, brown women who deserve to see their stories centered. SAINTS OF STORM AND SORROW comes out June 2024 from Titan Books.

AVRAH C. BAREN

Avrah (she/they) is a fantasy/ sci fi writer based in the DMV, where she lives with a neurotic tuxedo cat. She is an alum of the Pitch Wars Class of 2021 and a graduate of the Futurescapes 2023 Writers' Workshop. They spend their days researching trees and landcover change, which is probably why she mostly writes worlds with huge forests. They love writing fantastical tales with Jewish-coded and explicitly Jewish characters that explore our connections with nature and each other. When she isn't writing, she is thrift shopping, working at the Renaissance

Festival, and trying to become a wood witch. Find them on socials @avrahwrites.

ROSE REGEANT

Rose Regeant is a writer, cat mom, and very tired teacher. She lives in Florida with her wife.

VALO WING

Valo Wing is a recovering operatic soprano turned professional funeral singer. Their short fiction is published in *Haven Speculative, Cosmic Horror Monthly, Brigids Gate Press,* amongst others, and was placed on the 2023 Nebula Awards recommended reading list. They are a 2021 Pitch Wars mentee and 2022 Futurescapes Writers' Workshop alum. They live outside New York City. You can find them on socials @valo_wing.

ALISTAIR REEVES

Alistair (he/him) writes romantasy about messy queers and morally grey characters. Born in Canada, he moved to England to indulge his addiction to hot caffeinated beverages. His influences range from video games to Chinese danmei. When not writing, he can be found playing Dungeons & Dragons or tending to his frankly absurd collection of succulents. In 2019 he won a Watty Award for his queer science fiction, Static Crush, and was a 2022 Pitch Wars mentee. A SPELL FOR HEART-SICKNESS is his debut novel, releasing with Podium in Fall

2024. He graduated from Sheridan College with a Bachelors in Animation, but he mostly uses his artistic skills to draw his OC's kissing.

TALIA GREER

Talia Greer is the author of the paranormal monster romance novels Sasquatch Summer and Alder King Spring, and the romantic fantasy novel A Cure for Magic. She lives in the mountains with her gamer husband and two chaotic cat children. When she's not writing, she's drinking iced coffee or watching truly terrible horror movies. Talia can be found on Instagram and TikTok at @taliagreerbooks, and online at taliagreerbook s.com.

P.H. LOW

P. H. Low is a Locus- and Rhysling-nominated Malaysian American writer and poet whose debut novel, *These Deathless Shores*, is forthcoming from Orbit Books (US) and Angry Robot (UK/NZ/Australia) in July 2024. Their shorter work is published in *Strange Horizons, Fantasy Magazine, Reactor*, and *Diabolical Plots*, among others. P. H. can be found on Twitter/X and Instagram @_lowpH, and online at ph-low.com.

TB WRIGHT

TB Wright (he/him) is a writer of adult speculative fiction involving messy people making bad decisions. A software engineer by day and general tinkerer by night, he enjoys writing complicated queer characters in no-win situations, making sub-par bread, and drinking far too much coffee for his own good. TB can be found online on Twitter/X @tbwrightwrites and online at tbwrightwrites.com.

LILLIAN BARRY

Lillian Barry writes in short spells when the world stops spinning, which, when you have vertigo, isn't all that often. They write queer romance, including *The Santa Pageant* (2023; audio 2024). Lillian's non-bookish interests include playing brass instruments, watching anime, and getting sucked into the microcosm of a niche video game. A Channel Islander by childhood, they currently live in Ireland with their beloved partner. Find them @SoLillianBarry on social media.

www.ingramcontent.com/pod-product-compliance
Lightning Source LLC
Chambersburg PA
CBHW061535310726
48972CB00008B/2462